ZACK DELACRUZ

ME AND MY BIG MOUTH

ZACK DELACRUZ

ME AND MY BIG MOUTH

By Jeff Anderson

STERLING CHILDREN'S BOOKS
New York

STERLING CHILDREN'S BOOKS
New York

An Imprint of Sterling Publishing Co., Inc.
1166 Avenue of the Americas
New York, NY 10036

Paperback edition published in 2016 by Sterling Publishing Co., Inc.

ISBN 978-1-4549-2127-1

Distributed in Canada by Sterling Publishing Co., Inc.
c/o Canadian Manda Group, 664 Annette Street
Toronto, Ontario, Canada M6S 2C8
Distributed in the United Kingdom by GMC Distribution Services
Castle Place, 166 High Street, Lewes, East Sussex, England BN7 1XU
Distributed in Australia by NewSouth Books
45 Beach Street, Coogee, NSW 2034, Australia

For information about custom editions, special sales, and premium
and corporate purchases, please contact Sterling Special Sales at
800-805-5489 or specialsales@sterlingpublishing.com.

Manufactured in Canada

Lot #:
2 4 6 8 10 9 7 5 3
08/16

www.sterlingpublishing.com

Illustrations and design by Andrea Miller

To everyone who ever felt different.

—J.A.

CONTENTS

No snowflake in an avalanche ever feels responsible.
—**Stanislaw Jerzy Lec**

GYM WALL

ME

A typhoon spray of spit.
A stupid assembly.
And my big mouth.

That's all it took to ruin my life.

If you're a sixth grader at Davy Crockett Middle School in San Antonio, Texas, you start off every day in advisory. Besides cruel and unusual punishment, advisory is an avoiding game: avoiding eye contact, avoiding talking, and, so far, avoiding trouble.

So when a scratchy announcement ended advisory early for an anti-bullying assembly, my stomach gurgled. I'm not a fan of change.

I stumbled through the rusted metal door frames of the gym. Echoing laughter and shouts bounced off the hardwood floors. A sea of black, red, and khaki uniforms collected at the door as everyone looked for their friends.

Suddenly, my too-long, grow-into-them-soon khaki pants seemed even longer. My Harry Potter glasses felt bigger and shinier and dumber than ever.

I had to find Marquis fast. He's the only friend I'd made this year so far.

A whistle screeched in my left ear.

"Hey, fill up the rows back to front!" Coach Ostraticki yelled, holding a whistle in his hairy fingers. In middle school, coaches were always *yelling you* what to do.

Pretending to search for a seat, I kept looking for Marquis.

The whistle blew two quick bursts. "Delacruz? Sit!" He pointed his werewolf finger like I was a bad puppy who'd peed on his Nikes. If you asked me, Coach O. needed the anti-bullying rally more than we did.

I sat on the hard bleacher so I could keep looking in peace.

"Don't sit here, *Enrique* Potter," a kid with a gold earring said. "This seat is saved."

I stood.

Coach Ostraticki squinted sideways at me, threatening to blow his whistle again.

"Is this seat taken?" I asked a girl with pigtails sitting with Cliché Jones. Cliché is in a bunch of my classes, and she's never really been mean to me—but then again she's never really been nice either.

Pigtails stared at me like a statue till I moved along.

"Did you see his pants? That little boy needs to shop in the toddler's section next time," Pigtails said loud enough for me to hear.

"It's not mean if it's true." Cliché laughed.

I pulled up my pants, which immediately sagged down again.

A few rows behind them, I spotted an open seat on the bleachers next to the wall. I scooted sideways toward the spot, and a whoosh of cool air moved the gelled spikes in my hair. Perfect—an air vent and a wall.

I patted the cool wall with my hand and sat.

Hello, Gym Wall.

The fewer people to be near the better. A couple of days before, in technology arts, we had a sub, and for the whole period a seventh grader kicked my back. Once he kicked so hard, I blurted out a grunt and the sub wrote *my* name on the board for being disruptive. That's why I was sticking with walls. Walls never kick you or insult your clothes, and they always support you. In fact, I could lean on *Gym Wall*, and I did.

Yep, you've probably figured out bullying is a ginormous problem at Davy Crockett Middle School. The Fighting Alamos needed to be checked—fast. And how else would you solve any serious problem?

Have a forty-five-minute assembly.

But this anti-bullying assembly had to be better than the lame one in elementary. Who could forget *I am thumb buddy*? Nothing could be worse than a gym full of kids chanting, both thumbs up, "I am thumb buddy special! You are thumb buddy special too!"

Middle school was nothing like elementary last year. There, quiet kids walked school-zone slow in straight lines led by the teacher. Here, passing between classes was a zoo. Actually, more like a jungle—zoos have cages. At the "Home of the Fighting Alamos" sixth, seventh, and eighth graders roamed wild, loud, and free.

The enormous buzzing lights flashed on and off. I slouched down behind a guy who pulled up his hoodie. I kept scanning the crowd for Marquis.

"Toot! Toot! All aboard the Goodfriend Express!" a bleached blonde in hot-pink overalls hollered, chugging her arms like a train. Did she just say *toot*? Anti-bullying tip number one: Don't ask for it.

"I'm your conductor, Ima Goodfriend."

Okay, so it got worse.

Fast.

Thumb buddy should've warned me.

"Whooo-*weee*! Uh!" catcalled an eighth grader from the back of the bleachers. Howling and whistling filled the gym. This assembly was speeding off its tracks. I wondered who'd be the assembly victim this year. Everybody remembered what happened to Steve Ramirez when he was tricked into leading the "I am thumb buddy" chant in elementary. To this day, people still stick their thumbs up and yell, "You are thumb buddy *thpethi*al," every time he walks by. You just can't erase stuff like that. Ever. But I wasn't getting tricked into anything. I just sat with my buddy *Gym Wall*, hunching down behind the guy in the black hoodie. At least there was one good thing about being short.

Principal Akins tapped his white bullhorn. *SQUEEEEAL!*

Everybody's hands shot up to cover their ears.

4

"Stud*ens*." That's how our principal says *students*. Don't ask. The white bullhorn blocked his face except for his shiny forehead. "We need to seek to respect our fine speaker." *SQUEEEAL!* "You'll want to seek to open your ears to what she has to communicate to you."

Ima talked over the noise. "I am here to lead Davy Crockett Middle School to its next stop: A Goodfriend Express Bully-Free Zone. How's that sound?" Her voice echoed into the preacher mic taped to her face.

A low hum of *boo* rumbled across the gym. Teachers' heads whipped around with who–was–that? and you-better-quit-now looks.

"That's right. *Boo* to the bullies!" The train wasn't stopping. Ima leaned on a stool, eying the crowd with her Gatorade Cool Blue eyes. "Things are about to get real."

Whoa! This lady had some *loco* motives, if you asked me.

"Have any of you ever been . . . *bullied*?" Ima crossed the shiny wood floor toward the bleachers.

Who'd be dumb enough to raise their hand for that? I wondered.

"Back in the day, the kids used to say I had *summer* teeth. *Some're* over here, and *some're* over there."

Laughter rattled the bleachers.

"But I showed them." Ima grinned. "I got braces."

"Metal mouth!" a skinny kid with braces yelled from the front row. He quickly covered his mouth and sat back down. Seems like teeth are big bully magnets. Anti-bullying tip number two: Keep your teeth covered.

Then, Ima Goodfriend asked for volunteers to act out a scene for the Goodfriend Express Players.

Everybody froze. Nobody wanted to make any sudden movements that could be mistaken for volunteering. Plain and simple: no one wanted to be a Steve Ramirez. Ima scanned the crowd. Somehow she got two suckers—I mean, volunteers—to walk to the center of the gym floor.

A boy with a shadowy mustache held the microphone.

"Hi. My name is Rudy McRude." The boy read his lines flat as cardboard. "Uh, I don't feel good about myself, so I use put-downs all the time to make myself feel better."

Rudy passed the microphone to a girl with braids.

She grabbed it and held it right up to her mouth. *Wheeeeze huh! Wheeze huh!*

Great! A mouth breather.

Wheeze huh! She sucked in another deep breath and rushed through each line. "I'm Diana Different, and I am different." *Wheeeeze huh!* "I hope everyone at this new school likes me."

It was like she was diving underwater at gunpoint. Man, was I glad I wasn't up there. She was taking a bullet for the whole school.

"Hey! Diana Mouth Breather, you're taking our breath away!" I think the heckler was José Soto. He's in almost all my classes and always starting stuff.

Laughter spread through the gym.

Anti-bullying tip number three: Keep your breathing to yourself.

Ima knocked Rudy McRude's shoulder, so he droned on. "Um, you are different. Your clothes are not even cool."

Ima walked toward the bleachers. "So, what do you

think Diana Different should do next?" Ima stared at the crowd. "Turn and talk to the person next to you, and discuss a solution that will buy you a ticket on the Goodfriend Express."

The closest girl on my left turned away, so I spun back to the wall.

Hello again, Gym Wall!

Gym's favorite idea of mine was that Diana Mouth Breather should shove Rudy McRude in front of a train or bus or whatever came first. Gym agreed with me—as he often does, being a wall and all—that none of the other answers were as good as mine.

"Kids, the thing we often miss is Rudy McRude *wants* friends." Ima leaned forward. "He just doesn't act appropriately. Diana Different could ask Rudy McRude to sit at her table at lunch—or to sit next to her on the bus."

"What are you *on*, lady?" a boy yelled from a few rows over.

"I am *on* the Goodfriend Express." Ima talked louder and faster. "Join me, won't you? Be the caboose and get the Goodfriend Express on track. When someone is being bullied, back up the victim like a *caboose*!"

She threw her hands up and pushed out her caboose and started pumpin' and bumpin'.

"Back it up! Back it up!" she clapped, yelled, pumped, and bumped.

Mr. Akins stood quickly. "It's time we seek to come to a conclusion, Ms. Goodfriend." The lights lowered, and Ima turned to the projector.

"Let's end by being the caboose and practicing what to

say to bullies," Ima said, except she kept saying it *ca-booose*.

¡Mira! She was going to *train* us.

On the tiny screen, a fake train crossing sign popped up with a flashing *X* over the words *Bully Crossing*. A list of chants started scrolling.

We mumbled the list together: "Chug a chug, don't be a thug!"

Mr. Akins interrupted, tapping his watch, stepping toward Ima. He knew this assembly needed its emergency brake pulled.

Gee, I wanted to say the next one: *Train your brain to be humane*. Uh, wait. No, I didn't.

Ima held her one-more-minute finger up to Mr. Akins, who stretched out his collar like it was choking him.

Ima, the runaway train, told the entire gym to stand up.

"We're gonna get our rally on!"

We got off our *ca-booooses*.

"Are you ready to yell?" Ima said.

Mr. Akins paced, gripping his bullhorn.

"Let's do this, Crockett Middle School!"

And then something changed. I don't know if it was because we all knew Mr. Akins wanted *The Goodfriend Express* to stop, or that kids never passed up a chance to scream at school. Whatever it was, we all boarded her runaway train, and there was no turning back.

"No more bullies! No more bullies!" we shouted.

"Louder!" Ima encouraged.

We stomped our feet on the bleachers as we screamed. "NO MORE BULLIES! NO MORE BULLIES!!"

My stomping and shouting let out all the times this year I'd been called names or been kicked or had my binder shoved out of my hands.

"You be the change! YOU be the change!"

Even Principal Akins shouted in his bullhorn.

And I didn't plan it, but pretty soon I yelled the loudest. I stomped the hardest.

At that moment, my eyes caught a flash of Marquis's baby-blue warm-up jacket in the middle of the bleachers. He looked back. We raised our fists together and chanted, "I'll be the change! I'LL BE THE CHANGE!"

All the stomping and chanting became one movement, one voice, floating up, higher and higher, all the way to the skylights, rising and rising till the metal ceiling rattled.

I tilted my head back, and for a second I thought maybe things could change.

Then the electronic bell blasted, and the mob scattered like somebody had just called in a bomb threat. But I just stood there, students swirling around me like a kaleidoscope.

CHAPTER 2
A BULLY ACHE

SPIT MIST

I never planned to get on The Goodfriend Express, but later, in the library, I learned that you couldn't plan everything. Some things just happen.

The librarian, Mrs. Darling, sang, "I have a secret!"

No one looked up.

"And it has to do with you-hoo!" she sang louder and higher.

"We don't ca-a-are," José sang back, making a field goal in the paper football tournament at his table.

Mrs. Darling crossed her arms, pretending to pout. "Fine. Since you aren't interested in my secret, I suppose we should get down to business: the business . . . of words." She still held out hope we'd catch her disease for books. She didn't get that we didn't want to be like someone who drew on her eyebrows with a black Magic Marker, high up, always looking real surprised. Believe me, it was not one bit darling.

"Eyes on me, one, two, three." Her chipper voice sounded like a crazy fairy godmother fueled by a Rapstar Energy Drink. And all eyes were on everything else but her: white spitballs hit the ceiling, a group of girls dabbed on blue eye shadow, and a paper football flew between a two-handed goalpost.

But why their eyes weren't on her, I'll never know. Her hair, electric red, was not a color I'd ever seen in nature. Her dangly earrings, shaped like books, bounced when she got excited, which was all the time.

But Mrs. Darling's pyrotechnic love of words was not dimmed by our boredom. Holding up a sentence strip, Mrs. Darling revealed the word, *stupendous*, which was written with the same marker she used on her eyebrows. She tilted her head to the right and ran her hand beneath the strip.

"Who can pronounce this exquisite word?" Mrs. Darling cooed, her red mop of hair bobbing from side to side.

"Anyone?" Her green eyes widened, like in a low-budget horror film.

I sure wasn't going to say anything. If you answer questions, everybody called you schoolboy. Embarrassment to middle school students was like kryptonite to Superman.

Usually Cliché Jones offered an answer, but she was way too busy playing with the lace on the little white socks she always wore.

Chewy Johnson interrupted the silence to ask if he could go to the bathroom. Again.

Janie Bustamante was the only person raising her hand.

You have to know about Janie. Many of us have been in school with her for the last seven years, so we knew that in her mouth, the letter *s* multiplied, built up volume, then sprayed out of her mouth like a fire hose. Don't ask me why she'd even try.

She hoisted herself out of her chair and plowed down the aisle to where Mrs. Darling stood.

"SSSSSSStupendoussss!"

Spit sprayed from Janie's mouth, dispersing into a fine mist above the class.

"Incoming!" José dove under a table, leaving only the flashing red heels of his sneakers in view.

Mrs. Darling backed up against a wall of bookcases, trapped against nonfiction.

The fine spray widened in flight, like the sprinklers at the Villa De La Fountaine apartments.

Sophia, too busy separating her eyelashes with a paper clip, never even saw it coming. The spit cloud coated Sophia's arm and her long black hair like a toxic morning dew.

"Ughhh!" Sophia snarled, looking like an angry clown. Did I mention Sophia wears a lot of makeup? Well, if I said it five more times, it wouldn't be enough. *Enough* wasn't on Sophia's vocabulary list.

Sophia Segura was the only girl in sixth grade with an eighth-grade boyfriend. This would've been a bigger deal except this was Sophia's second time in sixth grade. Rumor had it that last year she stole a spoon from the cafeteria and stuck the handle in an outlet, blowing out all the lights in the sixth-grade hall. That's why we all have to use plastic Sporks now. Like Principal Akins says, actions have consequences. Anyway, let's just say she was not the kind of girl you want to coat with spit. Sophia oozed popularity, and a few girls would do anything to get some of it on them. But since spit wasn't popularity, her clique rustled in their bags, scrounging for tissues for Sophia.

Mrs. Darling's phone rang on the other side of the library.

"I bet I know what *this* is about," she sang as she walked behind the checkout desk to answer.

José leaped up to fill the dead air. "We still don't care!" He was always ready to go whenever an interruption happened. He was like a Comedy Central app that activated whenever an adult wasn't listening.

He's called El Pollo Loco—the crazy chicken. More like El *Bully* Loco if you asked me. Using his hollowed-out Bic pen as a microphone, El Pollo Loco began his comedy roast of Janie. "This chick brings a whole new meaning to 'say it, don't spray it.'"

The class burst into laughter.

Still on the phone, Mrs. Darling waved her hand at the class.

Somehow, somewhere, somebody decided José was cool because he made us laugh. I had to admit sometimes he was funny, but it felt wrong to laugh when José was being plain cruel. He was sixth grade's most popular entertainment. This was fine—as long as you weren't the punch line of his jokes.

José placed both hands on the side of his face, widening

his eyes. "Sssseriousssly! What do you think you are? A human sprinkler?" I waited for someone to stand up for Janie—to back her up like a caboose.

"Bustamante." Janie stood. "Janie Bustamante."

Okay, you also need to know Janie watches classic movies all the time. She quoted them whether it made sense or not.

"*Any* James Bond movie. Nineteen sixty-eight to the present." She bowed for imaginary applause and sat down.

After every famous movie line, Janie just had to tell you what movie it's from. She didn't know anti-bullying tip number one: Don't ask for it. And she sure didn't know the word *quiet*.

Unlike Janie, I knew *quiet*. The Discovery Channel would say I had adapted to survive. I didn't even get up to sharpen my pencil during class. I kept a little yellow sharpener in my front pocket, so I didn't have to walk in front of everybody.

"Janie, is it true that you were the reason they invented spit guards on salad bars?" José rocked his head back and forth, air boxing his fists toward her like an MMA fighter.

"I hate sssalad!" Janie yelled.

"I can tell!" José laughed. "Could she make this any easier, folks?"

I looked around the library. Maybe Cliché would back Janie up like a caboose, I thought. But she sat there, arms crossed, rubbing her arms like they were cold. Why wasn't anyone stopping this?

José kept the zingers flying. "I bet the only letters of the alphabet you know are KFC."

Janie stared forward, her brown eyes glazing over, ears reddening.

I should've stood up for her. But if I'd said something, it wouldn't be long before I was the one being embarrassed. For instance, since my name is Zack Delacruz, José called me Shrimp Delacruz—like a bad pun on the seafood dish Shrimp Veracruz you order at Mexican restaurants. I get it. I'm small. I'm Mexican. *Hi*-larious.

"Janie's face is like an onion"—José watched all the nodding faces—"because it makes me want to cry." He twisted his fists in front of his eyes.

I wondered where Janie's caboose was. When was it going to arrive? I knew I couldn't be the caboose. That would have been in direct violation of my plan to fade into the yellow cinder-block walls like scrubbed graffiti.

Ima Goodfriend had said: "Stand up when someone's being bullied. Be the caboose." Thing was, nobody ever did. Not before the anti-bullying assemblies; not after. I supposed everyone was relieved it wasn't them being teased.

Ima's words argued with me in my head: "*You* stand up. *You* be the change."

Janie looked around, her wet eyes asking, where is my caboose?

"Hey, I'm an explorer like in social studies!" José walked right up to Janie. "I just found a new continent."

This wasn't my problem.

"She's so big I don't even think Dora could explore her." José circled her.

Janie bowed her head.

"If she did . . ."

"Stop it, José!"

The room went silent.

Finally someone had the guts to be the caboose.

Everyone looked to see who had stood up for Janie Bustamante, the human sprinkler, the girl who recites movie lines and doesn't know the word *quiet*.

I was as shocked as anybody.

It was me.

CHAPTER 3
IN CHARGE AND IN TROUBLE

Everybody froze, eyes wide, mouths hanging open.

I eyed my friend Marquis for a clue on how to get out of this mess. But Marquis shrugged, playing with the zipper on his jacket, the whites of his eyes getting bigger and bigger.

Oh, so now he's shy. I knew that move. I invented it.

I avoided eye contact with José by staring at Marquis's zipper, wishing I could get everybody's eyes off me, one, two, three. Especially José's. I knew I was next in the roast lineup now.

Mrs. Darling stomped over and sang, "It's time to reveal the big secret!"

"I'll be back after a short intermission," José whispered, glaring at me like I owed him money.

"Is everything all right here?" Mrs. Darling asked, sensing a problem.

"Oh, it will be," José said, arms crossed, not taking his eyes off me.

What was I supposed to do? Tattle? Yeah, that'd work out well.

"Well, that was Principal Akins on the phone, and it's official. Sixth grade has a stupendous opportunity, and I've finally gotten approval to tell you." Mrs. Darling cleared her throat. "For the first time in the history of Davy Crockett Middle School, the sixth grade has a *chance*"— Mrs. Darling paused for *dumb-matic* effect—"to attend the seventh- and eighth-grade dance!"

"Oooh, I want to go to that," Cliché Jones said. "The theme is 'A Night at the Alamo.' That's so romantic."

Romantic? Did she remember what happened at the Alamo? It was a massacre. That was just one of the many problems of having a building for a mascot. All I remembered about the Alamo was that it was smaller than you think and it sat right next to River Center Mall downtown. Seriously. And in second grade, I got a coonskin cap at the Alamo gift shop.

I pictured the dance with a bunch of guys wearing coonskin caps, defending the Alamo with rifles while getting funky. It didn't seem romantic to me.

A spitball hit my neck and stuck. I didn't need to look; I knew where it came from.

But even José started listening once he heard *chance* and *dance* in the same sentence. Sixth graders had never been allowed to attend the fall dance. This was huge news. And better than that, everybody, including José, was *mucho* more interested in the dance than who stood up for Janie.

"The sixth graders get to go because of me," Sophia reported, pointing her chin up, watching us for our reaction.

Unlike me, Sophia didn't mind people looking at her. As her hoop earrings sparkled under the fluorescent lights, I wondered what it felt like to not be afraid of attention.

"My boyfriend, Raymond Montellongo, the president of eighth grade, came up with the idea so I could go with him." She flipped her hair back.

Raymond was actually president of the student council, but he might as well have been president of the school.

Sophia's clique clapped like trained seals.

"Be that as it may, I will be the faculty advisor for the sixth-grade fund-raiser challenge." Mrs. Darling grabbed the fringe lapels of her Pepto Bismol–pink jacket.

"And"—Sophia stood for this part—"we get to wear whatever we want." She looked around the room, nodding.

Everyone gasped like they'd just won the scratch-off lottery.

Wearing whatever we wanted was big news. At Davy Crockett Middle School, we are forced to wear a school uniform every day: black or red collared shirt with khaki bottoms.

"Sixth grade will be able to attend the seventh- and eighth-grade dance," Mrs. Darling continued, "on the condition that they sell forty-eight hundred dollars worth of Nation's Best chocolate bars in a week. The chocolate bars have been under lock and key in the storage closet at the back of the library, waiting for this very moment.

Everyone's head turned toward the closed closet doors.

"If every sixth grader sells at least one box of Nation's Best Chocolate Bars, then all grades will attend the dance for the first time."

"You had me at chocolate bars." Janie stood. "Inspired by *Jerry Maguire*, nineteen ninety-six, starring the ineffable Renée Zellweger."

"Inspired by chocolate, more like it," José said, "Am I right?" He punched Chewy Johnson in the arm.

Janie stuck out her tongue.

José stared at me to see if I'd dare interrupt him again.

Nope, Ms. Goodfriend, I was never cut out to be caboose material. This was my stop. I was jumping off the runaway train before it sailed off a cliff.

"I have a peanut allergy, so I can't sell anything with nuts," Cliché said, touching her stomach.

"Did you see on the news about the kid who got killed selling candy door to door?" Marquis asked, zipping his jacket nervously.

Cliché looked at Marquis and asked, "Who are you going to the dance with?"

He zipped even faster.

My stomach ached. I hoped everyone would keep talking. Soon they'd forget all about me standing up for Janie. Then I could slowly fade into the background again, a quiet avoider. Who was I kidding? José wouldn't stop. That was who he was—El Pollo Loco. His signature move was making people laugh, and mine was a big blank nothing.

"I bet Zack's going to the dance with his new girlfriend, Spiterella!" José pointed at me. "Maybe your dad can take you in that big orange Instant Lube van he drives."

How could José remember what my dad drove? Dad only dropped me off once in his disgusting bright-orange Instant Lube van. Why did bullies have to have such good memories about the bad stuff?

"Yeah, the orange van is like a pumpkin already!" Sophia high-fived José.

I crumpled into my chair like a wadded-up math test, shutting my eyes, trying to become invisible. But I soon learned that once you squeeze the toothpaste out of the tube, it doesn't go back inside.

"Aw, look, Zack is being all quiet. Is Janie the cocktail sauce to your shrimp?" José taunted. His mom works at Luby's Cafeteria, so he knows food. "Is she the liner lettuce for your platter?"

My stomach twisted. I was chum in the water, and the sharks were circling. The voices swirled around me. Maybe I could say something mean back.

Nope. I had tried that once at my old school, and it made it even worse. In fifth grade, on the playground at recess, a big lug named Auggie Sarabia shoved me to the ground. I stood up and tightened my fist.

"Don't even, runt!" Auggie yelled.

My tongue got bigger and filled my mouth. "Yeah, it flakes one to flow one."

Then everybody laughed harder and my face turned redder.

"Oh, he don't even know how to talk good." Auggie

pushed me down in the grass, staining my khakis and my reputation.

WWWWw

Mrs. Darling knocked me out of memory lane by flashing the library lights on and off to get our attention. But everybody kept talking, so she kept flashing—on and off, on and off. It looked like a club on MTV.

José lifted his hands above his head, jerked them back, and danced. The class giggled.

"That's awesome!" Sophia burst into laughter and began one of her near cheers: "Go, Loco, Go, Loco! Go, go, go, Loco!" Not a real cheer, but almost.

Even Marquis broke up.

I had to do something. And fast. If José could be cool by acting like the school fool, maybe I could get laughs too. I mean, my grandma always says I am funny enough to be on TV. Maybe my class just didn't know cool comic me, like Grandma did. Maybe if I danced even goofier, everybody'd think I was class clown instead of Janie's hero.

I went all in, pumping my arms up and dancing around like I was a Disney Channel stud. The class chuckled, so I popped and locked. When José noticed I was getting more laughs, he did the robot.

It became a dance-off.

Neither of us noticed that the lights had stopped flashing. Neither of us noticed that Mrs. Darling stood right behind us. When we did, I instantly knew why the class was laughing so hard. My comic dance career ended. Suddenly.

"Zack and José seem to be very *involved* today." Mrs. Darling's eyes widened, looking back and forth at us, like she was a witch and we were Hansel and *Ghetto*. Man, that lady had horror-movie eyes down.

"I guess you could say they're leaders."

Blood rushed to my face.

"Just what this project needs: people who can command attention." Mrs. Darling pushed us forward, her hands gripping our necks from behind—a bit too tight, I'd like to add. "Let me introduce you to my new helpers, the two young men in charge of the sixth-grade–dance fund-raiser: Zack and José."

CHAPTER 4
VOLUN-TOLD

The library fell so silent you could have heard Sophia's eyelash paper clip drop.

Well played, Mrs. Darling. Well played.

"They can't do it, Miss. José's funny, but he can't be in charge!" Sophia said, brushing her hair, which was now even shinier from the Bustamante spit conditioner. "And Zack"—she pointed her brush at me—"I didn't even know he was in this class till today."

"Now, now," Mrs. Darling interrupted.

"Yeah, I'm allergic to *shrimp*," José added, looking over at me. "Achoo-ee!"

"We must respect each other, and I know that these two fine young men will do a stupendous job being in charge." Mrs. Darling released our necks. "Gentlemen, stay in the library with me. The rest of you please line up to go back to class."

I know what's what. Teachers tell you you're real smart or a leader, so you can do their jobs for them. What do my mom and dad pay taxes for? "Oh, Zack, your writer's notebook looks so nice. Help Chewy organize his."

Whatever. Aren't there some child labor laws or something?

After our class left, Mrs. Darling leaned in. "Thank you two ever so much for volunteering." Her lipstick was smudged, making her look like The Joker.

"I didn't *volunteer*, I was *volun-told*," José reminded her, rubbing his neck.

"Mr. Soto, you volunteered when you came up to the front of the class, now didn't you? And what perfect people to lead the dance fund-raiser: two guys who know some moves!" Mrs. Darling closed her eyes, bent both knees, and tapped her foot to the left and then the right, rolling her arms and twisting her shoulders.

José and I froze in horror as Mrs. Darling did the old librarian version of the Dougie. It was like a car accident— you wanted to look away, but you couldn't. As Fresh D scooped her hip down lower and lower, a loud pop startled her eyes open.

"Miss." José patted her shoulder. "The Dougie is hip *hop*, not hip *pop*."

See? That was funny.

Mrs. Darling rubbed her hip. "I have something for the two of you to do, and it needs to be done pronto."

She waved for us to follow her to the dark storage closet at the back of the library.

Throwing the door open, she spun around slowly, her hand on her sore hip. "Ta-da!" Can I just say the storage room looked like a good place for an axe murderer to hide?

She clicked on the lights. Stacked from the floor to the ceiling were brown boxes. Boxes and boxes and boxes. On each box, NATION'S BEST CHOCOLATE BARS was written in navy letters. The stacks of boxes, arranged like a brick wall, were taller than me, taller than any of us. And somehow, I'd have to scale that cardboard-and-chocolate wall or be known for the rest of my life as the loser who stood up for Janie Bustamante *and* also ruined the dance for sixth grade.

Who was I kidding? I knew how labels stuck. Everyone knew what happened to Poops McGillicutty in second grade. I mean Bruce. See? Everyone was just one burrito lunch and a long gym class away from being Poops McGillicutty.

My stomach rumbled.

"This afternoon you will distribute all the boxes to the sixth grade." Mrs. Darling walked over and pointed at one of the boxes. "Each sixth grader should take at least one case. If they do, then by the end of next week, if all goes well . . . ," she sang, "you should be dancin', yeah!" Striking a pose, she pointed her right arm in the air.

Before I could get the words out to explain why I couldn't do this job, José beat me to it.

"Miss," José interrupted, "I'm feeling boxed in." Laughing, he slapped his knee.

Mrs. Darling wasn't falling for the comedy stylings of one El Pollo Loco.

And just like that, he became all business. "Look, lady, I don't know if you know this or not, but I'm not put in charge of nothing."

José winked at Mrs. Darling like they had an understanding. "I am sure Loser, pardon me, *Zack* Delacruz can handle this on his own." He glared at me.

Mrs. Darling's crazy eyes rolled around, letting him know that wasn't happening. "I am perfectly aware you haven't had the opportunity to demonstrate what good leaders you can be, but I can see from your energy and get-up-and-go, you will be perfect together."

She turned. "No more worries. Chop! Chop!" She picked up a can of Rapstar Energy Drink off the table and chugged it down.

Then she tapped on a heap of order forms and two pens. "Make sure you record who takes how much. Students will return the money this Friday, and *voilà*, sixth grade goes to the dance. Does that sound like something you can handle?"

How were we supposed to do all this in five days? That's insane.

"What if I say no?" I asked.

"I *am* saying no," José said, crossing his arms.

"We're all set then," she said. "The first class will be here in ten minutes. I'll check with you in a bit. Toodles!" Then, Mrs. Darling threw the Rapstar Energy Drink can over her shoulder, clanging it into the metal trash can in the corner. "Word to your mother!" She walked out the door without looking back.

CHAPTER 5
HAUNTED BY JOSÉ

The library storage closet was haunted. Story is, the first year the school was open, a kid racked up a load of library fines he couldn't pay. After mowing lawns all summer, he returned to school to pay off the fines. But they say he was never seen or heard from again. Except in the middle of the night, when moaning and the sound of books dropping to the ground can be heard.

I wished I could disappear like that boy right now, but instead I was haunted by something much worse than death: José. The only dropping sounds I heard were the boxes of Nation's Best chocolate falling over when José climbed on top of them.

"Pick them up, *Loser Delacruzer*!"

We were supposedly working on passing all the candy out, so we could be released from our chocolate bar prison.

I was working.

José was *supposedly* working.

"I am the supervisor, Shrimps," José said, atop the box wall, kicking his legs.

I wish I could tell you how fun it was to be out of class, how José and I became the best of friends because, in the end, he pitched in and did his part. He saw the light and was no longer a bully and stopped picking on me. But then I'd be a liar in addition to a bigmouth.

Being supervisor apparently meant El Pollo Loco made fun of people while I did all the work. Why couldn't I be partnered with somebody like my boy, Marquis?

By the time the third swarm of kids came in, looking at the lists Mrs. Darling gave me, I could see we had more cases than sixth graders left.

"Chewy," I said, "I can't give you a box because you have a library fine. It says so right here." I pointed at the highlighted line on the list.

Chewy nodded.

"How'd you lose a book?" I asked. "We've only been in school for a month."

"Well, I didn't lose it exactly." He shuffled his feet. "I kind of dropped it in the toilet."

"Hey, man, if you don't like a book, just return it. Don't give it a swirly." José hopped down from the boxes. "Can I have an amen?"

Somebody needed to drop José's jokes in a toilet. And hold them down. For a long, long time.

"Amen," said Chewy, his shuffling becoming the pee dance. "Is there a bathroom back here?"

"Bathrooms are for paying customers only, sir. Let me escort you from the premises." José shoved Chewy out of the storage closet door like a candy bouncer.

"What have we here?" Mrs. Darling said, holding two trays from the cafeteria in her hands.

"Uh." José shrugged. "Just keeping out the riffraff, ma'am. I don't know if you're aware, but that boy has a library fine." José dragged his finger across his neck like it was being sliced off. "Tsk! Tsk!"

"Oh, I am aware of more than you know, José." She winked at me and placed the trays on the table. "This will be a working lunch. The next class will be here in a bit. Keep up the good work, gentlemen."

I tried to call out to her, to let her know that we were going to have leftover boxes. I tried to explain that she never told me what to do with extra boxes. I wanted to tell her to take José far, far away. But my voice stuck in my throat like I had swallowed a whole packet of dry ramen noodles—all at once.

"I'm bored," José announced, sitting down next to me.

For José, a working lunch meant blowing milk bubbles, peeling the breading off his fish squares, and throwing it in my hair when my back was turned. To top things off, he stomped on a ketchup packet, which squirted all over. I got a paper towel and wiped red ketchup off the boxes. It looked like blood spatter at a crime scene. As I cleaned, I thought about how this would *not* be what I'd be doing if Marquis were my partner.

I met Marquis the second week of school. It was my first time taking the bus to Dad's apartment. I had been at Mom's the first week. I was feeling really scared. How was I supposed to stay stealthy if had to take one bus to Mom's house for a week and then another to Dad's apartment the next week? Kids would notice.

Even though I didn't want to switch buses, I had to.

I was avoiding getting on the bus. Slowly, I climbed the black rubber covered stairs of Bus 81. Marquis noticed me right away. He got up and walked over to my seat.

"You're Zack from English, right?" He sat.

"Um, yeah, I guess," I said.

"Well, I guess I'm Marquis then." He showed his white teeth. He was funny. That was the first thing I liked about him.

"Did you move?" Marquis asked. He was also nosey. That was the first thing I didn't like about him.

"No," I said. He was a real Cam Jansen, shooting questions at me like I was a mystery to be solved.

"Well, then why are you on this bus?" he asked.

"I'm visiting a sick friend," I shot back.

"Who?" he asked.

I couldn't think of an answer. This kid was good. Looking out the bus window I saw a McDonald's. "McDonald."

"McDonald?" He squinted. This kid was a dog with a bone. He wasn't letting go. "McDonald *who*?"

"Oh, you don't know him," I said.

"I might," Marquis said, "I've lived on this same bus route for five years."

"Can we talk about something else?" I said. "Talking about my sick friend upsets me."

Luckily, before I knew it, I had stalled long enough. We reached my stop, and I jumped up and said, "I gotta go."

The next day on the bus, he asked how my friend was. What was I supposed to do? This kid was going to keep on me for the rest of the year, so I said the only thing I could say to end the questions.

"He died."

"Oh," Marquis said. "My sympathies."

Marquis never accused me of lying that day or the next, even though I supposed he knew. He'd given me a pass, and my lie floated away like a loose plastic bag on the side of Highway 281. And it was replaced by friendship.

wwww

I stood up and threw away the ketchup-soaked paper towel when my daydream ended suddenly. The metal doors of the storage closet flung open and hit the wall so hard, they bounced closed again.

From behind the door, I heard a muffled voice. "I want three boxes!"

Janie opened the doors, a little less like Godzilla this time, and walked into the closet like she owned it.

"Hey, Janie, tell me the truth," José asked with a concerned look in his eyes, "when you get a cut, does gravy come out?"

I scowled at José.

"Oh, that's right," he teased, flipping up the collar of

his polo. "I forgot she's your *lay-day.*"

I handed three boxes to her, and she hugged them under one arm.

Janie moved toward the door, then turned and held up her fist.

"Wait for it . . . ," José said, eyebrows up.

"*As God is my witness, I shall nevah be hungry again!*" And then she was gone with the chocolate bars.

She stuck her head in just long enough to bring down the curtain. "*Gone with the Wind*, nineteen thirty-nine, starring Ms. Vivien Leigh and Mr. Clark Gable."

A fish square exploded on the door as it shut.

CHAPTER 6
ESCAPE FROM CHOCOLATRAZ

By the end of the day, six boxes were left. All that stood between the sixth grade getting into the dance were six boxes of Nation's Best chocolate bars.

"I figure that leaves three boxes for each of us, José."

"I'm not taking any boxes." José pushed his shoulders back. "I'm management. Call me Mr. Soto. You work for me, Shrimps." He thumped his finger on my chest. "Figure it out. Or else."

The bell blasted.

Boxless, José bolted out the door, scurrying like a rat escaping a sinking ship. Grabbing one box, I fled my candy prison before the bell finished.

"I'll lock up, gentlemen," Mrs. Darling yelled as we flew past. Maybe she wouldn't notice I didn't pass out all the candy bars. My mind ran three steps ahead of me all the way to the bus. Who would take the extra boxes? How would I be able to keep working with José?

When I got to Bus 81, I froze on the curb.

Worry banged around in my head like a tennis shoe in the dryer. I wasn't a salesman. I didn't even talk to people unless I already knew them. Talking to people was so embarrassing. What could I do? Knock on all the apartment doors at the Villa De La Fountaine? What would happen when that scary guy with the skull tattoos opened his door? He'd probably feed me to his pit bull.

There I was, standing at the bus loop trying to work up the courage to get on Bus 81. The whole candy-dance-Janie thing was giving me a headache. Speaking of headaches, Coach Ostraticki was walking toward me.

The little curlicues on the end of his mustache grossed me out and put me in a trance at the same time. It was like he had a trained scorpion on his upper lip. The little scorpion on his face did a dance while he bounded toward me in a head-to-toe purple warm-up suit.

"You." The mustache curls moved as he talked. "Stop loitering." How was I supposed to know what *loitering* even meant? I wasn't in college last time I checked.

After I slowly climbed the black steps of Bus 81, kids turned away from the aisle to face the window. They must've been afraid I'd beg them to take another box again like I'd done all day. I was about to tap Chewy Johnson on the shoulder to convince him to pay his library fine when Marquis yelled from the back of the bus.

"Zack, over here."

I walked back toward my friend. I plopped my chocolate bar box on the green seat between us and sat.

"What's up, my man?" Marquis smiled. "How's Candyland?"

My voice stayed stuck in my dry-ramen-noodle throat. "Zack?"

I took a breath. "There are still five boxes left, but nobody will take any more." I turned to him. "It's all on me."

"Well, I'd take more"—he tapped the box of Nation's Best chocolate bars in his lap—"but I already know Ma will only let me sell them to the old folks at Shady Groves Rest Home, where she works." Marquis lives with his grandma, but everyone calls her Ma. "She doesn't let me go out and knock on strangers' doors." Marquis shook his head. "No sir."

I rubbed the back of my neck.

"You'll figure it out, my man."

I nodded.

"You will!"

Once I got off the bus, I stood on the curb and waved good-bye to Marquis. His head hung out of the window, smiling like he didn't know my life had ended.

Poor guy.

He wouldn't know what hit him when I was gone.

Okay. I was being overly dramatic.

I waited as a jacked-up Chevy drove by, rap music blaring, shiny chrome wheels blinding me as the sun hit them.

I navigated the crumbling asphalt as I headed across

the street to Dad's new AD apartment. (AD was short for "after-divorce." It was like BD, "before divorce." My entire family life was forever separated by BD and AD.)

After two months, I was still trying to get used to this place. I stood for a moment looking at the apartment sign:

The Villa De La Fountaine Apartments, Fine French Living. Free Gas and Water, Move-in Special!

Yeah, it sounded like it could be kind of nice.

It wasn't.

The letters were fading and someone had put a gang tag over what used to be a picture of a fountain.

I had the key to Dad's AD apartment on a white string tied around my neck. "That way you won't lose it," Mom had said. Mom always got up in my business. Even on the weeks I didn't live with her she told me what to do.

The door creaked open. The living room and kitchen counter were stacked with boxes. Why can't I get away from boxes?! Was AD Dad planning on staying? I opened the pantry door: trash bags, Fabulosa cleaner, and an open-for-business Roach Motel. No tortillas or peanut butter. Boxes, boxes, everywhere, and not a bite to eat.

I walked around the counter to the living room. More boxes. No TV. Did I mention there wasn't a TV?

What were you supposed to do without a TV?

Seriously.

Dad only had the boxed set of the *Godfather* movies. I'd been watching that over and over on Dad's laptop till Mom found out and put an end to it. Gee, you have one bad dream about getting chased down by an angry gangster . . .

I wondered if I was on one of those extreme-survival shows, secretly being filmed. I spoke out to the empty AD living room, "Cut! I quit!" I made the time-out sign in the silence.

But no camera crew, no friendly hosts, no bright lights came busting through the doors. I supposed this was just how my AD life was going to be—not even interesting enough for a reality TV show.

I flopped down on the ratty brown couch that smelled like wet dog. Dad rented it with the apartment for an extra ten bucks a month. Personally, I thought they ought to be paying us for storage. Though it was better than sitting on a box.

These days my whole life stank like that couch: living in two houses, taking two buses, standing up for Janie, being put in charge of the fund-raiser with El Pollo Loco, a bully and a goof-off. It was enough to make a man tired. I stretched out on the sorry excuse for a sofa and rested my eyes for a minute.

Next thing I knew Dad's keys jingled in the door. Then a blurry Dad towered over me.

"How was school today?" he asked.

"When are we getting a TV, Dad?" I changed the subject.

"Hello to you too, Zack," Dad said.

I looked at the grease smudge on his gray coverall. It covered the C on his name patch, where it said *Carlos* in red letters over white.

"You know, Zack, I am not sure if we should even get a TV."

My heart sank.

Dad sat on the couch next to me and took off his shoes. He rubbed his beard, squinting his eyes. "Since the divorce, money is kind of tight."

It was like Raymond Montellongo had just punched me in the stomach. But this was Dad. First Mom made Dad move out. Then, I had to live with Dad every other week in a place that isn't even fit for living. He had promised we'd get a TV.

"I want to make some changes, Zack," Dad said.

He wouldn't stop. He just kept going. Dads are supposed to give kids everything they need, like TVs and snacks. And for crying out loud, dads' feet *aren't* supposed to stink so much. I stood up, clamping my nose.

"Why don't you change your socks?" I said.

"Very funny, Zack." He reached over and patted the

back of my leg. "I think we watch TV too much."

"Not lately. Not since we moved to the Villa De La Prison."

"Hey now, Zack." He moved in for a side hug.

"Dad, I want to make some changes too," I squirmed out from under his arm and stomped toward the door. My voice shook. "The first one is no more changes." And I slammed the door like an exclamation mark, telling Dad I was serious. Seriously mad.

I went out to get some fresh air, like Mom used to do.

I walked around the terraces—a fancy name for the railed, cracked-cement sidewalks outside the doors of the upstairs apartments. I searched for someplace to go. Anywhere but back inside.

I stomped down the stairs.

I wanted out.

I walked to the street, and then I turned around. I didn't really have anywhere else to go.

Finally, I slumped down next to the soda machine that hummed under the stairs. This is what I wanted—no more changing buses, no more changing houses and parents, and definitely no more soda machines that hum.

The soda machine made a kicking noise and the hum got even louder. I wished it was loud enough to drown out all the thinking in my head. I banged the back of my head against the machine.

I opened my eyes.

Dad stared down at me.

"Come inside, Zack." Dad offered his hand to me. I grabbed it and he lifted me up.

"Can I have a soda?" I asked.

"Is that what you're doing here?" Dad asked. "You know, Zack, you can't just bang your head on it waiting for something to magically come out. It takes a buck."

I smiled.

"Oh, what's that?" Dad tickled my waist. "Somebody's smiling."

"Cut it out." I pushed his hand away.

Dad reached in his pocket, took out his wallet, pulled out a dollar bill, and straightened it on his leg. "Pick what you want, Zack."

He handed me the dollar.

"It's all you." He touched my shoulder.

He got that right.

CHAPTER 7

NOTABLY FRIGHTENED

The next morning, when I walked into Mrs. Harrington's English class, Janie looked up and said in some accent, "Top of the morning to you, Zack."

I acted like I didn't hear her and plopped down in my assigned seat. *Ah! Something familiar,* I thought.

"Class, one of the most important skills you will learn in middle school is the power to persuade an audience to change their beliefs or actions." Mrs. Harrington balanced on her stool and continued reading from her teacher's edition script.

"Miss, can I persuade you to give us a free day today?" El Pollo Loco put his hands together like he was praying.

"To reach an audience successfully, you consider the current beliefs of that audience before you begin."

She didn't look up unless the teacher's edition specifically told her "look at the students."

While I was pretending to listen to Mrs. Harrington, Cliché Jones elbowed me. A folded-up piece of notebook paper slid across the desk.

A note?

It couldn't be.

No one had ever sent a note to me before.

Notes were for people like Sophia—popular people. I was the guy who looked at the dirty floor tiles while I walked down the hall. I wasn't popular, and I didn't get notes—and I would never ever be the kind of guy who got notes if I messed up this dance.

I double-checked to see if I was supposed to pass the note to someone else. But ZACK was written above a triangular flap in all capital letters, which told me to "pull here" in lowercase.

I sat up a little and unfolded the note carefully as Mrs. Harrington continued.

When I saw Janie's name at the bottom, I threw up a little in my mouth. Go-Gurt tasted even worse when it made a curtain call.

I looked around to see who noticed me getting the note.

Janie waved. Her smile revealed a chocolate-covered tooth.

And worse than that, everybody else was watching too—first Janie, then me—like some sort of tennis match. To me, to Janie. To me, to Janie. I wanted the score to be zero-zero, but they looked at the two of us like the score was love-love.

"Zack, have you written something you'd like to share with the class?" Mrs. Harrington asked.

"Uh . . ."

So now she looked up from the teacher's edition? Seriously? Did the teacher's edition tell her to *look for someone to embarrass*?

"Miss, Zack got a love note from his girlfriend, *Janie*," Cliché tattled.

The class laughed—except Janie and me.

"No!" Quickly, I stuffed the note in my front pocket. "She's not my girlfriend."

"Hey, I thought you said we couldn't have love notes." Sophia slammed her compact on her desk.

"It's not a love note," I whined.

It was happening again. The sharks were circling.

"Read it," Janie mouthed. At least, that's what I hoped she mouthed.

"Mrs. Harrington, you should read it to the class to punish them." José stood.

"José." Mrs. Harrington pointed to his chair.

"You just take my love notes because you are jealous of me, Miss." Sophia rolled her eyes.

"I am choosing to ignore that, Sophia."

There Mrs. Harrington went again—choosing to ignore things. She made it sound so easy.

I should've chosen to ignore everything. But Janie waved her arms, trying to get my attention. Her chair creaked every time she shifted. And everyone was still watching us. The more I ignored her, the more she would lean this way and that. I wanted her to stop, but as usual, Janie was unstoppable.

"It's like one of the *telenovelas* my *abuelita* watches," Sophia jeered. "True love always wins on the soaps."

Janie turned to Sophia and hissed like a cat, raising her hands like claws.

All the *s*'s at the end of the hiss gave Janie's spit a new momentum. Chewy and Marquis created shields by covering their heads with their writer's notebooks. Cliché popped out her pink Disney Channel umbrella just in the nick of time.

Then, Janie turned to me. "Zack, I need . . ."

"Hey, she *needs* you!" El Pollo Loco interrupted. "Your kids will be the spitting image of you!"

"Class!" Mrs. Harrington stepped toward us.

The laughter and voices garbled together, and I felt like I was underwater, sinking to the bottom of a deep pool. I wanted the brown tile floor to open up and suck me back to the world I was used to living in: a world where Janie Bustamante didn't smile at me or want my attention. A world where I wasn't in charge of getting the sixth grade into the school dance. A world where I didn't have to work with the school *cruel*-median. A world where I lived in one house with both parents who weren't too busy or too broke to help me fix all that was wrong with my life.

But the filthy floor didn't open. And neither did the note—*that* stayed in my pocket. I stared at the fake wood top on my desk, looking for answers in the twists and turns of the grain until the bell rang. I knew what I had to do next.

CHAPTER 8
CHECKED OUT

In the hallway, I tried to dart through the crowd like one of Coach O.'s obstacle courses, but the hall to the cafeteria was all backed up as everyone headed to lunch.

Before I could pass through, Sophia and her clique spread the rumor like a virus.

"Hey, Zack, how's your girlfriend? Did she invite you on a lunch date with her love note?" Sophia teased.

"I know, right?" one of her clique snickered as they circled around us.

Janie lumbered up, hugging her binder tight to her chest. "What do you say, Zack?"

"Oh, that's cute," Sophia taunted, "the hippopotamus is chasing after her itty-bitty baby, Zack."

"I know, right?" another member of the clique said. Again. I could see why there was only one clique leader.

Janie spun around to the blue-eye-shadow gang. "Don't you have some kittens you need to drown?"

Before they could reply, I called over my shoulder to Marquis, "Let's make like a tree, and leaf." I sprinted down the emptying hall.

In the pizza line, Marquis trotted up behind me.

Out of breath, I planted the note in Marquis's hand. "Please, read it for me. I just can't read it."

Marquis unfolded the note. "Oh." Marquis's eyes widened. "Dude."

"What?"

"It's a marriage proposal."

"What?" My body stiffened. "But . . ." In that moment, I was glad my mom had forced me to start wearing deodorant every day.

"Snap!" Marquis cracked a smile. "I had you there, didn't I?"

I snatched the note from his hand.

"It's not so bad; she just wants two more boxes to sell." Marquis picked up two plates with rectangular pieces of pizza from under the warming light, placing one on my tray and one on his.

I was relieved. All she wanted was *more* candy—more boxes of Nation's Best chocolate bars. She wanted candy—not me.

"You have to take a fruit," the cashier ordered.

I was so relieved to get rid of two more boxes, I didn't even argue with the hair-netted food Nazi. I picked up one of the "oranges" and dropped it on my tray with a thud.

Marquis and I walked to the table by the stage, close to

the lunch monitor. Mo' adults, less problems, I always say. At least in the cafeteria. That was Mrs. Gage's territory. She was the cafeteria's guard dog, sniffing out trouble.

"So I guess the candy problem is almost solved," Marquis pulled his chair out.

Two more trays plunked down at our table. It was Janie.

The buzz of voices lowered.

"Not quite," I mumbled to Marquis.

Faces around the cafeteria turned and watched. Even Mrs. Gage left her perch, leaning on the stage, to move closer. She crossed her arms.

I couldn't handle all the attention. And maybe I should not have bailed on Marquis, but I had to get everyone's eyes off me. "Janie, meet me in the library in five minutes." My chair scraped loudly as I pushed back from the table.

"Perfect," Janie said. "That gives me plenty of time to eat."

I passed tables of smirking faces.

As I walked toward the cafeteria door, the buzz rose again.

That's right, folks, nothing to see. Just trying to get y'all a dance.

⁓⁓⁓⁓

A few minutes later, when I walked into the library, Mrs. Darling peeked over the lime-green half-glasses she wore on a chain.

"I am here to pass out two more boxes." I grinned.

"My hero," Mrs. Darling said, placing a hand over her heart like she was pledging allegiance to me. "Truly."

"Yeah." I looked at the piles of pink overdue slips in front of her. "Can I have the keys to the tomb?"

"Yes, you may, Mr. Delacruz." She took the keys off her wrist with a flourish. "What a great leadership role you have taken on. I knew all along you'd rise to the occasion."

I nodded.

She was right, I guessed. I was rising to the occasion. I had gotten almost all the boxes checked out. But how on earth was I going to get rid of the last three? Nobody wanted them.

I unlocked the doors to the haunted storage room for what I hoped was one of the last times. The five boxes— all that was left of the great wall of chocolate—waited for Janie.

"I'm here, Zack." Janie barged into the closet.

I looked at her. "Thanks for the good work, Janie."

She smiled. "It's my pleasure."

I couldn't believe Janie had turned out to be the best salesperson. Without her, the sixth grade would never get into the dance. It was nice not to feel like everything was all on my shoulders. Janie was doing her part. More than her part, really.

I lifted the two boxes to the table.

"You know, Janie, you can hand in your money for what you've already sold. You don't have to carry it all around. We collect money every morning in the cafeteria."

"I know." She peeked around the table. "I've got it under control. So, are those three boxes all that you have left, Zack?"

I nodded.

Janie stared at the boxes behind me. "Zack, why don't I just take the rest of the boxes?"

I wanted to throw my arms around her, but what if somebody saw?

"Uh. Are you sure? I mean . . ." I shook my head. "Sure. Yeah. Take the rest. Please." I leaned over and grabbed the last three boxes before she could change her mind.

I couldn't believe it. I really was rising to the occasion. Thanks to Janie.

I felt taller.

Maybe I couldn't hug her, but I could give her a firm handshake. I stuck my hand toward her.

Janie looked down at my hand and slowly reached hers toward me. We shook a few pumps before both of our hands dropped.

I scrambled to stack the last five boxes, one after the other, in her arms.

"Thanks again, Janie." I patted the top box.

"I'm just backing you up. Like a *ca-booose*!"

We giggled.

"I never thanked you for what you did, Zack. Nobody ever stood up for me before."

"No problem," I said, which wasn't really true, but what was I supposed to say?

Balancing the boxes, she chugged toward the door like some kind of chocolate bar express. If she made it to her class without dropping her cargo, it'd be a miracle.

But right then, I thought I might believe in miracles. Because of Janie Bustamante. It was hard for me to believe, but the candy might all be sold soon. The sixth grade might actually go to the dance.

If that wasn't a miracle, then nothing was.

CHAPTER 9
SECRETS AND SURPRISES

I ran along the bus loop in front of the school, heading straight for Bus 81. I didn't even slow down when Coach Ostraticki blew his whistle at me.

"Give me a break!" he shouted after me. "No running!"

I took the bus steps two at a time. My head was up as I stepped down the aisle. I was smiling.

"Is this seat taken?" I asked Marquis.

"Yes." Marquis motioned to the empty space beside him. "By you."

You have to love Marquis. I hardly took a breath as I told him how Janie picked up the last boxes and how Mrs. Darling said nice stuff and how we were almost home free.

"I bet your dad will be proud of you, Zack."

"Oh." I looked out the window of the bus. "I never even told him about the candy or the dance."

"Maybe you should." He bumped my shoulder with his.

The bus jolted as it went over a pothole.

We sat in silence for a minute.

"I'm glad you're my friend, Marquis."

He smiled back, nodding. "Me too."

The squeal of the bus's brakes announced my stop.

~~~

The door of Dad's apartment was open a crack when I got to it. I knew Dad wouldn't be home from the Instant Lube for at least another hour.

Robbers? The hair lifted on the back of my neck.

Mom had never passed up a chance to remind me how Dad's new neighborhood wasn't "desirable," which is real-estate code for dangerous. Dad says Mom speaks in code a lot. She told me if I ever found myself in a "situation," I was supposed to yell, "Stop! I don't know you! Help!"

Yeah, that didn't seem right for this "situation."

Frozen, I stood in front of the black door with a gold 229 on it.

The door squeaked open, and I spun around to run from the robbers.

"Come on in, Zack," Dad said.

My shoulders dropped. I turned around. In the doorway, Dad stood smiling, already changed out of his uniform and in shorts and a T-shirt.

"I thought I'd take the afternoon off." He pushed the door the rest of the way in. "I've got a surprise for you."

The living room carpet was covered with white Styrofoam packing blocks, tons of clear plastic, a split-open cardboard box, cords, and a brand-new flat-screen TV.

"This is the new one with a touch screen." My voice got higher and higher. "I thought we couldn't afford it."

"Well, what are credit cards for?" Dad wadded up some of the plastic and stuffed it into an empty box.

"You sound like Mom."

"Don't remind me." Dad laughed. "I'm still paying for that dream house she wanted."

I helped Dad lift the flat screen onto two boxes he had put together to make a TV stand.

"Let's hook this puppy up," Dad said.

"Sure."

By the time we finished setting up the TV, we were starving. Since the fridge was empty, as usual, we drove across town to Chris Madrid's. That was our favorite hamburger place because they had the Cheddar Cheezy Macho Burger that was as big as my head.

Seriously.

It was like three pounds: huge hamburger patty, mustard, lettuce, tomatoes, onions, pickles, and an orange skirt of melted cheddar cheese hanging off all the edges. They didn't even make a bun big enough for the macho burger, so it all fell out when you ate it. It didn't come on a plate because it wouldn't fit. Instead they served it on a big plastic tray that caught everything that fell.

I had been trying to finish the whole macho burger ever since we started going to Chris Madrid's. Dad promised if

I ever did, he'd buy me the T-shirt that says "I ate the Macho Burger at Chris Madrid's." Mom hated the way people always fought over tables like gang territory, so it's always just been Dad's and my special place.

That night, I had only four or five big bites left on the grease-stained tissue paper.

"You put a pretty big dent in that thing." Dad jutted his chin at my tray. "Got some appetite on you."

"I've been doing a lot of stuff at school." I wiped some mustard off the side of my mouth with a napkin.

"That so?" Dad tossed his wadded-up napkin on the empty tray. "That's good news."

I leaned back in the chair and looked around. The restaurant was lit by tons of neon signs that hung every couple of feet above a wallpaper of dusty political T-shirts.

"Dad, you know how you always say you want me to be more involved at school?"

"Yeah?" He smiled, tilting his head.

I ran my hands along the broken mosaic-tile tabletop. It felt slippery on the bright tile and rough in the stained grout. "I'm in charge of the candy sale for the whole sixth grade."

"What?" Dad's mouth fell open. "When did this happen?"

"Yesterday."

"Oh, so when were you planning to tell me?"

"I don't know." I ran my hands along the rough grout. "I just wanted to be sure."

"Sure of what?"

"Are you done, sir?" An old lady in a dark-green apron

reached between us.

I wanted to say leave the burger, I'd finish it, but I couldn't eat another bite so I nodded.

The waitress stacked our trays and wiped the table, leaving behind the smell of bleach.

"I just wanted to be sure it would all work out and stuff." I sipped my Coke.

"So, you're sure now."

"Pretty much." I twirled my straw.

"I'm proud of you. I always knew you'd be a businessman."

"Can we watch something when we get home?"

"Sure." Dad hit the table with his hands and stood up.

"Can we watch *The Slash of Titans* again?"

"Titans. The job you never come home from," Dad said, imitating the voice from the commercial. "Come on, son." He squeezed my shoulder. "Let's go home."

We crossed the street to the parking lot.

"Dad," I said, pointing, "the moon looks like a toenail."

"You know, it does." Dad unlocked the van door on my side. "It sure does."

On the drive home, I rolled down the window of Dad's Instant Lube van. The fall air rushed over my face. Dad looked over at me, nodded, and turned up the radio.

I'd give anything to go back to that moment, even for a minute.

CHAPTER 10

PUNCTUATION MADE ITS MARK

It was three days into the sixth grade's Nation's Best chocolate bar fund-raiser, and my worrying had begun to fade.

In the cafeteria each morning, kids lined up to turn in their money, and Marquis would help me check them off the list. José was too busy "helping out with customer relations and motivating the sales force"—which apparently meant roaming around the cafeteria asking kids if they were going to eat their Pop-Tarts or drink their chocolate milk. It was hard to believe that such a skinny kid could eat so much.

To tell you the truth, I was glad José was roaming around. At least this way he wasn't torturing me about anything.

When sixth graders turned in their money, a few of

them called me Zack—not Shrimp or Loser or That Short Kid. I thought about asking Dad to measure me because I felt like I had grown. If not inches, I was starting to feel less afraid of everything. Not needing to avoid everything or worry about everything. Now I was in things.

"All we need is Janie and two other sixth graders to turn in their money tomorrow"—my numbers man, Marquis, slid a mechanical pencil behind his ear—"and we'll be set, boss."

At that point, even I was sure we'd have the whole thing wrapped up by Friday. Even Mr. Numbers backed me up.

"I reminded Mr. Akins to make the announcement that tomorrow is the last day to turn in the fund-raiser money," Marquis said.

I smiled at him and patted him on the back. "You da man, Marquis."

"You know that's right," Marquis said, collecting his papers.

"Seriously."

He stopped and looked at me. "Thanks. You da man too."

The bell rang and we rushed to math, Marquis's favorite class.

wwwww

Later that day, we walked into English, but for some reason everyone stopped at the door before they entered.

"Hey, Miss." Sophia looked suspicious. "Why are *you* wearing a dress?"

I did a double take when I saw Mrs. Harrington. That day, instead of her untucked faculty polo shirt and a khaki skirt, she wore a red dress with a black collar. It even looked like she had brushed her hair.

"Why are you so dolled up, Miss Harrington?" Cliché raised her eyebrows.

"Today is . . ."—Mrs. Harrington couldn't contain herself—"National Punctuation Day! Ladies and gentlemen, grab a pen and pick a punctuation station."

The class looked different too. The rows were gone.

Punctuation stations were everywhere. Four desks were pushed together with big laminated punctuation marks hanging over them: question marks, colons, periods, semicolons, dashes, quotation marks, and exclamation marks. Everything.

"This way, Zack." Marquis grabbed my arm and led me to the empty station by the window: the colon.

"It takes guts to start with the colon, boys," Mrs. Harrington snorted.

Sophia and Cliché waved their hands from the exclamation point station.

"Miss, we used *explanation* thingies in our sentence," Cliché said.

"Ex*clam*ation points!" Mrs. Harrington yelled. Punctuation must've been the Rapstar Energy Drink of language arts because Mrs. Harrington was hyper.

"Whatever." Sophia tossed back her hair behind her shoulders, cleared her throat, and shouted: "I can't wait to go to the dance!"

"Fantastic, Sophia!" screamed Mrs. Harrington,

jolting the class again. "Exclamation points are for extreme excitement or YELLING!"

"Yeah!" Cliché screamed a little too loudly, jumping up from her chair. "Sophia will dance cheek to cheek with RAYMOND!"

"Can I yell something out, Miss?" Chewy asked, squinting.

"Well, you're at the question mark station; can you?"

"Mrs. Harrington, can I go to the restroom?!" he shouted, then broke down giggling and wiping his runny nose. "Can I say anything that's *not* a question?"

"Will you?" jumped in Mrs. Harrington. When she moved her hands, I noticed her fingernails were painted red. It was like she wanted to date punctuation.

Chewy's legs were folded. "No, seriously, Miss, can I go to the restroom?"

She nodded, and Chewy sprinted to the door.

Janie Bustamante was at the comma station—alone. What did kids hate more: Janie or the comma? It was a toss-up.

"No one else wants to *pause* for a comma today?" Mrs. Harrington joked, smoothing her red dress. "This is a group activity, Janie. Why don't you join Marquis and Zack at the colon station?"

"*I want to be alone,*" Janie mumbled.

Something was different about Janie today. She seemed off. More than usual.

"The boys are glad to have you." Mrs. Harrington looked to us.

"Yeah, I know *Zack* is," José taunted, his eyes burning a hole in me.

Janie stomped over.

Like Ima Goodfriend, Mrs. Harrington didn't get middle school students. She was all peace, love, and understanding. Middle school wasn't any of those things. Did she think everything was good because we'd gone to a forty-five-minute Goodfriend Express assembly on Monday?

Frowning, Janie slammed herself down in the chair next to me.

"Zack and Janie, sitting in a tree, k-i-s-s-i-n-g . . . ," Sophia cheered with pencil pom-poms.

"*Explanation* point!" Cliché yelled.

Mrs. Harrington desperately searched her notes for something to distract us. *Hurry, Mrs. H., hurry!* I thought. I ran my hand over my spiky hair.

El Pollo Loco sprang up from the period station. "The branch broke off. Zack was crushed. Then came a medic in an am-bu-lance."

I slumped down in my chair so much I almost slid under the desk.

"I'm glad you're at the period station, José," Mrs. Harrington said as she crossed her arms, "because you. Need. To. Stop."

For the first time, the class honestly laughed at one of her lame English teacher jokes. But all the laughter, all the wild behavior had spoiled her super-special English teacher day for good.

She slipped off her black high heels and shook the heel of one of them at us. "And you *all* need to stop, class," she warned through gritted teeth. "Or we can take a punctuation quiz. Period."

She parked herself behind her desk and started reading her e-mail, not looking back at us. That was how a teacher let you know she was done with you.

Even though Janie had sold the most boxes of Nation's Best chocolate bars on her own, this whole thing about Janie being my girlfriend was destroying me. All I could think about was how on one hand, she was saving my reputation by selling candy, but on the other hand, she destroyed it by making everybody think we were a couple.

Just then, Janie slid another note to me.

Great.

I prayed no one had seen it.

I shoved it in my pocket and stared out the window at the cars in the teachers' parking lot.

The rest of the class was an ellipsis . . .

CHAPTER 11

DEATH OF A SALESMAN

Dear Zack,
I had an accident

s the bell blasted, Marquis and I dashed into the hall and made a beeline for the bathroom. Since we were lucky enough to be the first ones in, Marquis held the door closed with his foot. I wanted to open the note in private. I'd already been embarrassed enough today for a lifetime. Period.

After I skimmed Janie's note, I froze. All I could do was gaze ahead. The strong smell of dried urine punctuated my last moment as the kid who got the sixth grade into the dance. I handed the note to Marquis. "Read it. And please tell me my eyes aren't working. Please tell me I didn't just read what I think I did."

Keeping his foot turned sideways against the door, Marquis twisted and took the crumpled note. He grimaced as he looked at it and then read it aloud:

Dear Zack,

I had an accident with all the boxes of Nation's Best chocolate bars I checked out. I will need to check out new ones. Let me know when I can meet you in the library to pick them up.

Thanks,

Janie ☺

P.S. I need them A.S.A.P. !!

"New ones?" Marquis's face scrunched up.

I didn't have time to answer. The door shoved open and twisted Marquis's foot, knocking him to the green-and-white tile floor.

Chewy Johnson jumped over Marquis like a hurdle in gym class and headed for the long metal trough.

I kneeled. "Are you okay, Marquis?"

In the background, it sounded like Chewy was cleaning the metal urinal with a power washer.

"I think I twisted my ankle," Marquis grunted. "Bad."

"What?"

"My ankle." Marquis winced. "Help me, Zack!"

I could feel the exclamation point.

I could feel my whole world coming to an end.

Period.

El Pollo Loco ran into the bathroom and stepped over Marquis. He looked down from the other side. "Urine trouble." He held his stomach. "Get it?"

After I lifted him off the floor, Marquis used my shoulder like a crutch to limp to the nurse's office. Each step, Marquis flinched, gasped, or grunted.

Mrs. Harrington spotted us hobbling down the hall. "Here, take my rolling chair!" That's like a teacher giving up her firstborn child. They don't do that for anything other than a real emergency.

And it was Janie's stupid note that had caused the whole emergency in the first place. In fact, I would never have been put in charge of the dance if it weren't for her. This was all Janie's fault. And to think, I was about to forgive her, believing she'd saved the dance singlehandedly. But I knew the truth: she was ruining it, just like she wrecked everything. Even Marquis's ankle. My mind fumed all the way to the clinic by the main office.

When I opened the clinic door, Sophia stood at the sink rubbing ice over her lips, staring at herself in the mirror. She was the last person I wanted to see. I take that back; *Janie* was the last person I wanted to see. I wanted to Hulk out on her.

"What have we here?" Nurse Patty said.

"Hey, Shrimps, what happened? Did your girlfriend step on Marquis's foot or something?" Sophia giggled.

"You. Off to lunch." Nurse Patty waved her hand at Sophia, like she was a gnat buzzing around her clinic. "Now."

"Why, Miss?" she whined. "I wanna stay. I barely got here."

"Because I have to find out what put . . ."

"Marquis," I said.

"Marquis in this makeshift wheelchair." Nurse Patty squeezed Marquis's hand.

Marquis winced.

"Oh, dear." Nurse Patty looked at Sophia. "Out!"

Sophia disappeared.

Nurse Patty and I moved Marquis out of the chair to the clinic bed. I explained how Chewy had shoved the bathroom door open and twisted Marquis's ankle.

Janie burst in. "I need my Pepto-Bismol!"

"You will have to wait over there, Janie. I'm busy."

"Nobody puts Baby in a corner!"

"I do." Nurse Patty headed out the door to the file cabinets in the front office.

Janie stood in the corner and whispered to herself, "*Dirty Dancing*, nineteen eighty-seven, starring Mr. Patrick Swayze."

Oh, man, I thought. *Get this girl out of my face.* I was about to run her over with the Goodfriend Express. Chuggah, chuggah. To think, I stood up for her.

"Zack, I've been looking for you. Did you read my note?" Janie rocked on her feet in the corner.

"I've got bigger fish to fry now." I pointed to Marquis. "Look what you did, Janie!"

Janie stepped back. "But I . . ."

"What happened to all the boxes, Janie?" Marquis grunted.

"There was an accident," Janie said, turning away.

My stomach dropped. "Tell me everything, Janie!"

She pulled her hair behind her ear.

"JANIE!"

She breathed in and swallowed hard.

"What *kind* of accident?" I lowered my voice.

"An *accident* accident. That's why it's called an accident, Zack." She ran her fingers along the clinic's white counter. "I didn't do it on purpose."

"What do you mean, Janie?"

"What I said, Zack." She faced me. "I need to replace my boxes of Nation's Best chocolate bars."

"But what happened to all the ones you signed out?"

"They're gone." Janie stared forward, rubbing her arms. She flopped down on the end of the mint green vinyl bench next to Marquis.

"Did you lose them?" Marquis tried to lift his head.

"We can help find them." He collapsed and closed his eyes.

"I know where they are," Janie said as she stood, "but they're gone."

"Where's the money?"

"Well . . ." Janie played with the glass jar of tongue depressors on the counter.

"Janie?" My voice got louder each time I spoke.

"I accidentally . . . ate them."

"You ate all eight boxes?"

Janie gripped the counter edge. "I only ate them one chocolate bar at a time." She gasped.

And like that, the lights went out on the sixth-grade dance.

CHAPTER 12

NURSING OUR WOUNDS

"Put this ice on his ankle, and I'll be back in a minute," Nurse Patty said. The clinic door clicked shut.

I held the blue ice pack on Marquis's ankle.

Lying face up on the clinic bed, Marquis cracked open an eye to operate his mental calculator. "I figure eight boxes, with twelve chocolate bars in each box, at two dollars per bar," Marquis shifted his ankle, "brings you to one hundred ninety-two dollars."

Thank goodness for Marquis, my personal calculator of doom.

"You don't have to go all mathematic on me, Marquis!" Janie sprayed. "In the movies when kids tell the truth, everything works out."

"Oh, you're *right*, Janie." I rolled my eyes. "This is a movie." I grabbed a handful of the tongue depressors from

69

the counter.

"It's called 'The Creature That Ate the Sixth-Grade Dance'!" I threw tongue depressors at the floor, one after the other, punctuating my words: "One. Chocolate. Bar. At. A. Time."

I dumped the rest of the jar on the clinic floor. "Look, I accidentally dropped all these tongue . . . these tongue . . ." I was so mad I couldn't even say the word.

"Depressors," Marquis added, eyes still closed.

Janie kneeled and collected the tongue depressors off the floor, returning them to the jar.

"You know, Janie. You have to pay for all the boxes of candy you ate," I said.

Janie slumped. "I don't have . . ."

"One hundred ninety-two dollars," Marquis grunted.

"One hundred ninety-two anything. Well, I might have that many unicorn stickers, but I already stuck them on my dresser and they aren't coming off anytime soon. Trust me."

I paced.

"I think we might have a hundred ninety-two cans and even more bottles," she said hopefully. "My dad doesn't recycle."

"Yeah," I said. "What about your dad? Maybe you could ask him for the money." But I already knew her dad wouldn't help us. Mr. Bustamante was one scary dude. I remembered him picking up Janie in third grade. When the classroom door opened, Mr. Bustamante looked like he had just broken out of prison. His coveralls were tied at the waist and he wore a tank top, so everyone could see all his tattoos.

Janie stuck her head between her legs, muffling her voice. "Lately, Dad hasn't been getting any jobs. He'll just get mad and say I'm eating him out of house and home."

What could you say to that?

Seriously.

"Can I do some work?" Janie sniffed.

"What are you talking about Janie?" I turned. "That's what got us into trouble in the first place. You were supposed to be working by selling cases of Nation's Best chocolate bars. Not eating them."

"But you're in charge, Zack. With El Pollo Loco. Mrs. Darling said you were a leader." She placed the jar of tongue depressors back on the counter. "You have to help me, Zack." I didn't like it, but I knew she was right. But I couldn't see any way sixth grade was going to be part of the dance anymore.

~~~~

I rolled Marquis out into the warm afternoon sun.

"We'll figure something out, Zack," Marquis said, squinting.

His grandmother was already waiting in front of the school, her black Lincoln still running. She shook her head at us.

I opened the door and helped Marquis from the chair to the front seat. I watched them drive down the street. Away. I waved good-bye, thinking about the disaster I was in. No Marquis. No Nation's Best chocolate bars. No money. No dance. No ideas.

And Dad thought I had the whole thing under control. He hadn't been the same since Mom made him leave. Last night at Chris Madrid's he was like BD Dad instead of AD Dad. I couldn't disappoint him.

I sat in Mrs. Harrington's rolling chair on the sidewalk in front of the school.

An ant was crossing the cement sidewalk to the asphalt parking lot with half a Cheeto on its back. It looked huge in comparison. Instead of a Cheeto, I carried the fundraiser for the dance, which was too big to hold up. I leaned over the front of the chair and watched the ant cross over the curb.

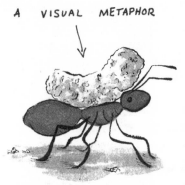

A VISUAL METAPHOR

I rolled myself slowly into the building, moving the chair with my feet like I was paddling upstream. I rolled to the clinic door. I couldn't face seeing the other sixth graders yet, knowing what I knew. Nurse Patty didn't even look up from the forms she was filling out as I rolled into the clinic.

"Are you waiting for me to stamp your frequent visitor card, Mr. Delacruz, or did you sustain an injury loading Marquis into his car?"

I rolled the chair around in a circle.

Nurse Patty twisted her head over her shoulder. "Okay, five more minutes"—she pushed her glasses up her nose— "but then it's back to class, sir."

"Yes, ma'am."

"Manners will get you far in this world, Mr. Delacruz."

Well, there was that, I guessed.

I searched the clinic for something to take my mind off this *candy-tastrophe*. I scanned the pamphlets to the left of Nurse Patty's door. Arranged in a little clear plastic rack, it was like a huge colorful quilt of sicknesses.

I spotted a pamphlet that said TOO MUCH on it. That sounded about right. This was too much. I rolled to the rack and grabbed it. I looked at the cover. Wait. This pamphlet was for addiction. We learned about this in health. The more I thought about it, the more eating eight boxes of Nation's Best chocolate bars in a week sounded like addiction.

"Gathering some reading material, Mr. Delacruz?"

"I think I found one for somebody I know. Can I take it?"

"That's what they're there for." She scratched her signature on a form and put it in a file.

I started reading through the glossy pamphlet. After reading some of it, I fist pumped the air. "Yes!"

I had always known something was wrong with Janie. This was proof.

I stood up, folded the pamphlet in half, and slid it in my front pocket. I quickly rolled the chair back to Mrs. Harrington's classroom.

CHAPTER 13
TOO MUCH

That afternoon, I clicked on the light in our apartment at Villa De La Fountaine. My stomach had been growling on the bus, so I headed for the pantry: trash bags, Fabulosa cleaner, and a jar of Dollar-Store Pe-*nutt* Sandwich Spread. (Yes, that was how *peanut* was spelled. I guessed you couldn't legally call it peanut butter unless it had peanuts in it.)

Anyway, it had been a take-the-jar-with-you kind of day, so I grabbed the fake peanut butter and a clean spoon. I took the silver phone off the charger next to Dad's bed. He wouldn't be home from work for at least another hour.

Sitting on the edge of the unmade bed, I pulled the pamphlet from my pocket and unfolded it. I unscrewed the lid of the "peanut butter" and dug a heaping spoonful from the jar. While I ate, I stared at the cover of the *TOO*

MUCH pamphlet. The organization's name was spelled out with words:

THE
ORGANIZATION OF
OVER-INDULGENCE
MEETINGS AND
UNITED
COALITION
HELPLINE

At the bottom, I found the phone number: *Call 1-555-TOO-MUCH and speak to a qualified psychiatric technician.*

I dialed.

After three rings, that recorded-voice lady answered, "Have your problems become . . . TOO MUCH? Hello, this is TOO MUCH: the addiction helpline. If you want to continue in English, please press 1."

So I did.

"If you are a health professional or health care provider, please press 3."

I didn't.

"If you're in need of immediate help with a life-threatening matter, please hang up and dial 911."

I couldn't.

I knew to stay on the line. I had called 911 a few years ago when the cable went out. Let's just say I learned that "life threatening" had a very specific meaning.

With the spoon, I burrowed out another mound of Pe-nutt Spread.

TOOMUCH

THE

ORGANIZATION OF

OVER-INDULGENCE

MEETINGS AND

UNITED

COALITION

HELPLINE

CALL 1-555-TOO-MUCH
AND SPEAK TO A QUALIFIED
PSYCHIATRIC TECHNICIAN.

Every few seconds the recorded voice lady came back and said how important my call was. I kept studying the information in the pamphlet.

Finally, the voice said, "Thank you for waiting. If you are over eighteen and want to speak to a counselor, please press 4. If you're under eighteen, please hang up and call back with an adult on the line with you."

What?

I was already in too deep. But I wasn't going to let a little thing like not being eighteen stop me from getting help.

My finger hung above the 4 button.

"To hear the menu again," the voice insisted, "press the pound key, or press 9 to hang up."

I lightly traced the edges of the 4 button with my finger.

"Are you still there?"

The voice was getting downright bossy. It practically forced me to press the 4.

"You're now being connected to a TOO MUCH specialist. For quality assurance, your phone call may be recorded."

"Good afternoon," a gentle voice said. "This is Amanda. May I help you on the road to recovery?"

The spoon clanged when it dropped on the metal bedside table.

"It's okay," Amanda encouraged, "I was where you are once. You've taken the first step. You placed this phone call, which means you're ready to be helped."

"Oh, it's not for me."

"Oh . . . I see."

"It's a friend."

"Okay. A *friend*. What's this *friend*'s name?" Amanda said *friend* all in italics.

"She's not really a friend, but her name *is* Janie," Two can italicize, *Amanda*.

"Okay, let's call her *Janie* then."

"That would be good, because *that's her name*."

"Of course it is. What are *her* problems?"

"Janie ate all of the Nation's Best chocolate bars that she was supposed to sell for the dance fund-raiser—eight boxes."

"Are we really talking about chocolate bars?"

"Yes."

"So, *Janie* ate all the chocolate bars, and now she feels out of control."

"Exactly," I said. "The problem is she doesn't have the two hundred bucks to pay for what she ate. Now the whole sixth grade won't be able to go to the Night at the Alamo dance unless you help me figure out a solution."

I picked up the spoon from the table and then ate a whole spoonful of fake peanut butter all at once.

"You're really upset," she said.

I tried like heck to swallow it.

"Well, yeah, they're going to blame it all on me." My voice was muffled by the gunk in my mouth.

"Are you eating right now?"

I froze. "No."

"What's your name, sweetie? Are *you* Janie?"

"No!"

"What's your name then?"

I worried TOO MUCH might be tracking me down, and I wasn't eighteen, so I'd have to go to jail. Last time the 911 operator warned me that I could be prosecuted, and I didn't know exactly what that meant, but all words that end in "ooted" are bad: tooted, booted, electrocuted. I dropped the empty spoon on the carpet and leaped up.

"Mrs. Darling!" The words left my mouth before I could grab them back.

"Are you eighteen? If you're under eighteen, you must call with a parent or guardian."

I paced.

"Yes, indeedy." I spoke as high as I could, making a last-ditch effort at Mrs. Darling's voice. I tried so hard I ended up sounding British for some reason. "Right-o."

"Is your mom there?" Amanda asked.

"No, my parents just got a divorce, and Dad's still at the Instant Lube."

I gasped.

I had told her facts about me. And they weren't Mrs. Darling facts. What had I done? Amanda must've been some kind of addiction special agent.

"Is that what you are upset over? Your parents' divorce?"

"No." I paced faster. "I mean, yes, I mean, no . . ." I lifted the blinds to see if the SWAT team was racing into the Villa De La Fountaine parking lot.

"Calm down. You've come to the right place, Janie."

"I'm not Janie!" I dropped the blinds.

"Of course you're not," Amanda said. "Now, let's put

first things first. We need to talk to your mom or dad. When will your dad be home? I can call back."

That was it.

This lady was doing all she could to keep me on the line, acting all sugary sweet just so she could put a trace on the call. I watched TV. I knew how it all went down. I bet her name wasn't even Amanda.

"Janie, you should really call back with your dad or mom . . ."

It was all TOO MUCH.

"Um . . . I think I dialed the wrong number. I was trying to call the Golden Wok for takeout. *Sorry!*"

I hung up.

And to be sure no one could trace the call, I ripped the battery out of the handset and unplugged the charging station.

I grabbed the jar of Pe-nutt sandwich spread off the bed and knelt to get the spoon off the carpet. I wiped the spoon on the edge of Dad's sheet. I walked to the living room, turned out the lights, and slid down the living room wall to the carpet. Sitting in the dark, I finished the jar.

DOOMED

I didn't know if my stomach hurt because of all the worrying—or from all of whatever was actually in fake peanut butter.

I got off the floor to throw away the empty jar and noticed Dad's laptop sitting on the kitchen counter. I remembered TOO MUCH had a website.

I powered up Dad's computer, even though I wasn't supposed to go online when he wasn't there. But it was an emergency. He'd want to help me if I ever told him my problem. But I couldn't let Dad down. I had to fix my problem on my own.

I pulled up the TOO MUCH website on the laptop. The Internet never asked how old I was.

The colorful web page filled the screen with purple flowers and green fields, while piano music played from the speakers. I clicked on the Solutions link near the top of the page. Solutions were what our Mr. Gonzalez called the answers to math problems.

According to TOO MUCH, the best way to solve addiction problems was to have an intervention. I didn't know what an intervention was, but there were more links, like a PDF version of *Intervention Tips for Teens*. Perfect.

I decided to copy the tips down—fast. I had to shut off the computer before Dad got home in a few minutes. I skimmed the guidelines for interventions. The first thing was a checklist, "Is It Time for an Intervention?" The first item on the checklist said often addicts don't see their problems, and they don't realize they need help.

Check.

"Is their addiction causing pain for them and others?"

Check.

"Do they ever lie about their addiction?"

Check.

If you had more than three checks, the quiz said it was time to move on to part two: The Intervention. That was basically family members and friends ganging up on the addict, so they'd know a lot of people think they had a problem.

I wasn't Janie's friend or family member, but I was the leader. I didn't even know who Janie's friends were. She was always by herself. And we couldn't invite her dad, that was for sure. But for an intervention, we needed some people to show how she was giving everybody problems.

I scratched down as many notes as I could.

When I finally looked at the clock on the microwave

in the kitchen, I realized Dad would be home any second. I ran to the kitchen counter and put the computer back exactly where I'd found it. I placed my notes in my math book and started thinking about who could come to the intervention.

wWMm

Later, Dad took me to get supplies to make a poster for health, which was really an Intervention Tips poster for tomorrow. And honestly, getting the dance was for health. Mine. After we got home, I started thinking about who'd come to the intervention. El Pollo Loco would be there. After all, he was *supposedly* 50 percent responsible for this sale. And I needed help.

When I got home, I took the phone to my room and called Marquis.

Ma answered. "Zack, Marquis is doing his math homework, so he can only talk for a minute, okay?"

"Yes, ma'am."

"What's up, Candy Man?" Marquis chuckled.

"Okay, I think I have a solution to save the school dance for the sixth grade."

"My foot's fine, by the way," Marquis said. "Thanks for asking."

"I'm sorry. How's your ankle?"

"I'm just kidding, Zack. It isn't broken. Just sprained. I have to be on crutches for a few weeks, though."

"Are you coming to school tomorrow?" I asked.

"You can count on it."

"Good," I said. "Because I need your help."

"With the missing money mess?" Marquis asked.

"Kind of," I said. "I think I figured out what we can do."

"Good, because I think I'm gonna ask Cliché to go to the dance with me."

"Seriously?" Marquis and I had never really talked about girls before. "When did this happen?"

"I've been tutoring her in math class and," Marquis paused, "I think she kinda likes me."

"And you like her too?"

"I think I might."

"Careful, Marquis, I think she wants you for your division."

"You know that's right. My charm is multiplying." Marquis laughed.

"So how are you going to ask her?"

"I haven't worked out the equation yet," Marquis said.

I had never asked a girl out before either, so I didn't really know what else to say. After a long pause, I said, "Enough about you and your love life. We've gotta get to work." I kicked my legs off the edge of Dad's bed as I talked.

"All right, everybody wants a piece of Marquis. Are you going to ask your dad for the money?"

"No way," I said. "He so proud of me now. I don't want him to find out how I messed it all up."

"I hear that. So what's the plan, Candy Man?"

I lay across the bed. "Well, I've been doing some research online, and I learned there is only one solution for Janie."

"What?"

"An intervention."

"Huh?"

I shifted onto my side. "An intervention is this thing where a bunch of people get together and tell somebody like Janie how their problems are causing other people problems."

"You mean like a peer mediation?"

"Yes." That was it. "Exactly like a peer mediation." I'd worried how Mrs. Darling would feel about an intervention, but now it's just a peer mediation.

"How's all this going to help save the dance?"

I sat up. "When we tell her how she hurt us or the dance or whatever, Janie listens to us. And the website I found says she'll realize she has a problem, and she'll do something about it."

"Like what?"

I fell back on the pillow. "One day at a time, Marquis. It says so at TOO MUCH. They promised that if you deal with the disease first, everything else will fall into place. I'll call José," I said. "You call everybody you can—Sophia, Cliché, anybody. Explain all about the peer mediation and tell them to show up at the library at lunchtime, and I'll take care of the rest." I acted like I believed it would work, but I wasn't so sure. But what choice did I have?

"Whatever you say, my man. You're the one in charge. I'll start calling."

CHAPTER 15
OH MY DARLING

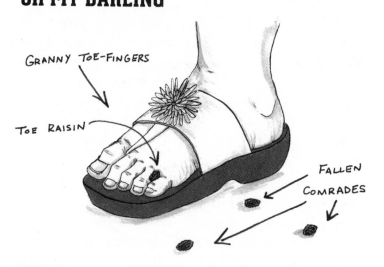

GRANNY TOE-FINGERS

TOE RAISIN

FALLEN COMRADES

You look tired, Zack," Dad said, gripping the wheel of his van.

Morning had come too soon. You know how sleeping on it is supposed to make things better? Well, it didn't work this time.

"Zack, you know I am proud of all the work you're doing." He put on his blinker. "I talked to your grandma last night and told her how proud I am of you."

Dad checked his rearview mirror.

I wanted to spill my guts. I wanted to tell him everything. I wanted to ask him what I should do. Because I didn't really have any idea. I wanted to ask him for the money, so I wouldn't have to get this whole intervention thing to work. I just wanted him to fix it all.

"We're all proud of you for stepping up, Zack."

I stared at the oval Ford sign on the navy glove box. "You okay?"

"Oh yeah, Dad. I'm just thinking of all I have to do when I get to school." Which was true. But mostly I had a sinking feeling this whole intervention thing was never going to work.

I stared at my reflection in the side mirror on the door.

The orange van pulled into the circle at the front of Davy Crockett Middle School.

By the glass doors, José bounced around like a total spaz, throwing raisins in the air and rushing forward or back to catch them in his mouth. Even without an audience, this kid was always on. I still don't get why he gets to be cool. When I opened the door to the van, I startled him. He jumped against a brick column and fell to the ground.

"What's wrong with him?" Dad rubbed his beard.

"There isn't enough time." I slammed the door.

As I turned toward José, a raisin landed on the spikes of my hair.

"So why do we have to talk to Mrs. Darling?" José's eyebrows squished together. "Mom was all suspicious of me coming early. I've never been to school early in my whole entire life." El Pollo Loco snatched the raisin lodged in my hair and popped it in his mouth. "Is this how you become a loser? Come to school early?"

"Just come with me." I slipped my backpack over my shoulder. "I'll do the talking." I pulled open the door to the school.

"Good, because I don't know what we're doing."

The fact was, I wasn't that sure either.

In the hallway, El Pollo Loco followed a few steps behind me, tossing raisins in front of us and then running up to catch them in his mouth. A few times he actually caught the raisin, but mostly he didn't. Instead, he left a trail of raisin droppings behind us that would make Manny the custodian think we had rats.

I shook my head and wondered why I even called him in the first place.

When I opened the library door, a raisin catapulted in before us and soared though the air, landing on Mrs. Darling's foot. That day she wore sandals, even though she shouldn't. Her toes looked like long, curled-up, old-people fingers. The raisin settled between her pinkie toe and the rest of the finger toes.

She didn't even notice the raisin invasion.

"Gentlemen," she cleared her throat, "to what do I owe the pleasure of your fine company so early this crisp fall morning?" She peered over her pink half-glasses. I swear she changed her glasses more often than some people change underwear. "Are you here to finish up some final paperwork for the sale?"

"Well . . . ," I said, distracted by the raisin between her nasty toes.

"Yes?" She waited.

I couldn't concentrate. All I could see was the stupid raisin between her talons.

"Are you pregnant?" El Pollo Loco tilted his head to the side.

"Pardon?" Her Magic Marker eyebrows rose.

"Are you pregnant?"

"José, you don't ever ask a woman that question," Mrs. Darling said, the raisin quivering as she took a step away from him.

"Yeah." I elbowed him. "I was going to do the talking,"

"Well, she looks pregnant."

"José!" I snapped.

"She does."

He was going to ruin this thing before it ever got started.

José shook the empty raisin box over his mouth. No more raisins.

"Mrs. Darling, a student at this school needs our help," I said.

José roamed behind the library checkout desk.

"What's happened?" Miss Darling stepped closer. She led me to the reading couch, and we sat. In the background, we could hear the loud tearing sounds of José making fake fingernails with book tape, which we chose to ignore. I was getting the hang of this ignoring thing—especially when it came to El Pollo Loco.

I explained everything:

The eating of chocolate bars.

"Oh, my." Mrs. Darling touched her hand to her chest.

TOO MUCH.

"Ohh, *myy.*"

How we needed a place to hold the peer mediation today at lunch.

"Ohhh, *myyy.*"

Mrs. Darling was speechless, so I acted like she'd already agreed to have the peer mediation in the library.

Mom told me it's the bread and butter of real estate sales talk. Assume the win. Act as if.

"That's all we need." I scooted to the front of the couch. "So we'll have the peer mediation meeting after third period? We'll set it all up right before. You won't have to do a thing."

"Well, I must say you're a very resourceful young man, Zack," Mrs. Darling said. "I love a man who does research."

She crossed her leg. The raisin must've attached itself to her toe finger because it stayed there. I nodded as I watched the raisin hang on for dear life.

"You've hit a bump, but it sounds like you're acting decisively, as a leader should. Sounds like I knew what I was doing when I put you two in charge."

"GRRRRR!" José clawed at us over the checkout desk with his book-tape fingernails.

Mrs. Darling cleared her throat and put her feet flat on the floor. That raisin wasn't going anywhere.

"Indeed, this is a bit unconventional, but you're certainly taking the bull by the horns." Mrs. Darling's eyes looked glassy. "I am touched by your caring for Janie, a peer in need."

Sliding on his stomach, El Pollo Loco crawled under the checkout desk. "GRRRR! GRRRR!" He was lunging his claws toward Mrs. Darling's toes.

"Is the human centipede going to be at the peer mediation?" Mrs. Darling shook her head side to side.

I nodded yes as I moved toward José.

"Ohhhh, *myyyy*."

I dragged José away from the counter—out of reach of Mrs. Darling's toe. He growled the whole time, by the way.

The first period bell rang.

I yanked El Pollo Loco off the floor before he could get the toe raisin.

"See you at lunch, Mrs. Darling. Thanks again!"

With both hands, I pushed José out of the library before Mrs. Darling could change her mind.

"Don't push me, man, or you're gonna be Zack Dela-BRUISE."

As soon as we entered the hallway, Principal Akins grabbed José's skinny arm.

"Seek to pause and declaw, sir."

I booked it to advisory without looking back. I knew the more distance I kept between José and this intervention the better.

All morning, I rehearsed in my head what I'd say at the meeting—through advisory, math, social studies. I had worked out exactly how I'd trick Janie into coming to the library for the intervention. You were never supposed to tell the addict you were having an intervention. They wouldn't come. You told them whatever you had to in order to get them there. It was about saving her life. (I think TOO MUCH gave me a run for being the most overdramatic.) I figured I'd tell Janie right before the intervention began. That way, she wouldn't have time to change her mind.

In a flash, it was third period—go time.

Walking into English, I took a deep breath and walked toward Janie's desk.

"Aw, look at that, Shrimps is making a beeline right over to his girlfriend." Sophia shook her head. She turned to her clique and whisper-yelled, "He better fix this dance thing. Raymond said if he doesn't, he'll hang him from the goalpost on the football field."

"Like a piñata," one of the clique said. "I wonder if his belly is full of candy."

Gulp.

Raymond Montellongo, the only eighth grader with a full mustache, was built like a Lucha Libre wrestler, and in the hallway he towered over all the other kids (and a few of the teachers). I had overheard our math teacher, Mr. Gonzalez, say they were going to put in Davy Crockett Middle School's first student parking space for Raymond.

Leaning toward us, Sophia tried to listen.

"I've got the help we need to make your chocolate bar problem go away," I whispered. "Don't go to lunch today, just come straight to the library."

"I have to go to lunch today, Zack." Janie shook her head no. "It's Burrito Thursday." Janie was not whispering. "I have been waiting since last Thursday." Burrito Thursdays were like a holy trinity of school lunches: the bean, the cheese, and the tortilla. Nothing came between kids and their burritos. I forgot that.

"Janie, that's your disease talking." My plan was already falling apart.

"Huh?"

"Nothing, Janie. Your burrito will be there," I lied.

"Promise?"

"Of course."

The intervention, I mean peer mediation, was happening just in time.

"You can do that?" Janie squinted her eyes at me, suspicious.

"Janie, I'm the leader, right?" I threw my hands out. "So follow."

The tardy bell rang and made me jump.

"Zack, you need to take your assigned seat," Mrs. Harrington said, walking to the front of the class.

I headed to my desk. Mrs. Harrington began explaining how we were going to write a persuasive letter today. I thought I'd write a letter to my parents persuading them to move me to a new school before this whole chocolate-bar-dance thing exploded in my face.

CHAPTER 16
TALKING IN CIRCLES

It was less than ten minutes before the lunch bell, and Marquis still hadn't come. I wondered if Marquis couldn't get the slips from Mrs. Darling. Maybe she changed her mind.

Mrs. Harrington's classroom door creaked open. Marquis, on crutches, hobbled into English class with a stack of slips and a note.

"What's this?" Mrs. Harrington put her hands on her hips, bunching up her polo shirt. She read the note, sighed, then thumbed through the slips.

Marquis winked at the class and smiled. If it was possible to rock a sprained ankle and crutches, Marquis was doing it. At least somebody was calm.

Sophia pulled a brush through her long hair.

"Ms. Segura, this isn't a beauty shop," Mrs. Harrington

said as she signed each slip.

"Uuuugh!" Sophia slammed her brush on the desk.

Why couldn't everybody just be good for one day? Was that too much to ask?

"Mr. Delacruz, Mr. Soto, Miss Jones, and . . . Miss Segura, please come up here."

They were the only people Marquis and I could get to come to the intervention. But that wasn't going to stop me.

"Why isn't tubby coming?" Sophia whispered, pointing her lip gloss toward Janie.

I put my finger over my mouth, shushing Sophia. "Don't worry, I've taken care of it."

We scooted out the door toward the library.

As we rounded the first corner, Sophia announced, "We need to freshen up."

Before I could say anything, the girls disappeared behind the door of the girl's bathroom. Marquis caught up, and we waited outside, leaning against the cool cinderblock wall.

"Hey, Marquis," I said. "Thanks for getting the notes taken care of."

"You're so grateful you left me in your dust." Marquis's eyes widened.

"Let's not get in trouble before we even make it to the library. Nobody can be mean to Janie. We need her to listen. We are trying to help her solve her problem so we can have a dance."

I looked at the clock in the hall and sighed.

"Maybe they're in the bathroom eating Sophia's makeup, so they can be pretty on the inside," José said.

I shouldn't have laughed, but I did.

Mr. Gonzalez's door creaked opened. "Boys, what are you doing out here?"

"Going to a peer mediation meeting, sir," Marquis said.

"Shall I call Principal Akins to help get you there?" Mr. Gonzalez flicked his hands away. "You're disturbing my class."

"No, sir, we're going," I said.

The girls were giggling and talking as they came out of the bathroom.

"*Shhhhh!*"

"What?" Sophia whined. "I want this to be fun."

We walked down the hall, and I tried to get them all in line. "Look, this isn't for fun. But if you want to have fun at the dance *later*, we have to be nice to Janie *now*."

I pushed my shoulders back. "Remember, it's all for the dance. No more calling her names."

José stood up. "Yeah, she's got a lot on her plate. Literally."

The girls giggled. I had a sinking feeling this was never going to work. What was I thinking?

"Listen to Zack!" Marquis yelled from behind, huffing to keep up, his crutches squeaking. "You want a dance, don't you?"

"We will, Marquis." Cliché stopped and looked back at him, batting her eyelashes.

Even Marquis was distracted from our job here.

Finally, we made it to the library without being stopped.

Sophia waited for me to pull open the library door for her. "Why are we here before Janie? I thought we were going to do that gang-up-on-her thing, that *invention* thing?"

"Intervention." I opened the door. "And we're going to call it a peer mediation now. We have to get ready for it fast." I followed them in. "And we aren't exactly ganging up on her."

"What do we have to do then?" Cliché whined.

"Don't worry, it's not math." Marquis grabbed a chair and started moving it, using it like the walker my grandma used. "All we have to do is put the chairs in a circle."

After they moved a total of two chairs, Sophia and Cliché sat in them, side by side.

"Where is the hippo . . . I mean, *Janie* sitting?" Sophia grinned. "I don't wanna be too close, right?"

Cliché raised her hand to ask a question, and Sophia gave her a high-five.

"Nice or no dance!" I warned. I put the last two chairs in the circle. Mrs. Darling could've called this whole thing off before Janie got here.

Mrs. Darling walked out of her office, finishing a pear. "Greetings, fellow peer mediators." She tossed the pear in the garbage can about ten feet away. "Soon we will get this peer mediation on the road." She wiped her hands on a paper towel. "Remember, we need to take Janie's feelings very seriously . . ."

I guessed she was planning on sitting in on the intervention. I thought this was "peer" mediation.

The library door swung open.

We all spun around expecting Janie.

Nurse Patty entered, squinting her eyes, holding up a piece of paper toward Mrs. Darling. "I got your note about the peer mediation." In her white jacket and comfortable shoes, Nurse Patty looked like she belonged in a hospital. She was the only one who might've known what she was doing. Was she going to try to run the thing?

Mrs. Darling walked to the circle and sat. "Thank you, Nurse Patty, we needed a medical professional to round out our circle." She tapped on the chair next to her, inviting Nurse Patty over with a wave. Looking as if the blue plastic chair would burn her, Nurse Patty sat.

"Zack has done some careful research and will be leading this meeting, but first I must warn you, ladies and gentlemen." Mrs. Darling paused. "Serious matters deserve serious attitudes. I think this is wonderful how you care so much about a peer."

Nurse Patty started to stand up to leave, but Mrs. Darling gripped Nurse Patty's arm and pulled her down into her seat.

"Zack has explained to me that we are going to try to help Janie." Mrs. Darling let go of Nurse Patty. "Janie is our concern here."

Nurse Patty rubbed her arm.

"Zack, go over those guidelines for the peer mediation you mentioned." Mrs. Darling waved her hand toward me and settled into her chair. "Let's put on our listening ears."

"These are the guidelines." I felt everybody was looking at my too-long pants. It was hard to breathe, but it was go time. Stiffly, I pointed to the poster I'd made last night. I'd copied notes off the PDF from the TOO MUCH website. It wasn't plagiarism though. I mean, I crossed out intervention and wrote "peer mediation" above it. I used my own words—like when it said him/her I only wrote her. And if I put the website I got it from on the poster, it was okay.

It took a while, but I read each of the tips on the poster to the circle.

PEER MEDIATION
7 ~~INTERVENTION~~ PRE TIPS FOR TEENS

- **BE GENTLE AND CARING. THIS Y CAN'T DO TOO MUCH.**
- **DON'T BLAME TOO MUCH. YOU DON'T WANT THE TEEN TO LEAVE.**
- **REMIND THE TEEN YOU CARE ABOUT HER, BUT YOU WANT HER TO GROW UP SAFELY.**
- **EXPLAIN HOW WORRIED YOU ARE AND HOW THE TEEN'S ACTIONS AFFECT YOU.**
- **BE SPECIFIC.**
- **BE FIRM.**
- **THE PERSON WHO THE ~~INTERVENTION~~ PEER MEDIATION IS FOR MAY NOT TALK UNTIL EVERYONE ELSE HAS SPOKEN.**

"Janie will be here in a minute. We are supposed to follow these rules for the inter—the peer mediation to work." Even though it was hard for me, I looked everyone in the eyes, even Sophia. "If we want this dance to happen, the first problem we have to solve is Janie. I mean"—I shook it off—"we have to help Janie solve her problem. Um, you know what I mean."

"I still don't see how this is going to get the money back," Sophia interrupted.

"Well, Sophia," I read off my notes, "in recovery we say, 'First things first.' Take care of the people first, and the rest will take care of itself."

Mrs. Darling beamed.

"Whatever, Shrimp Delacruz, but you better get us this dance, or I've got two words for you: *Ray*-mond." After mentioning her hulking boyfriend, Sophia bobbed her head back and forth like she was about to take off her earrings and jump me herself.

"Sophia, do you really think you'll be able to stay?" Mrs. Darling asked.

"Yes, Miss, I can." Sophia crossed her arms.

I had to make this work. I had everybody here. All that was missing was Janie. I checked the clock. I stood up. I sat down.

"Have you asked anyone to the dance yet, Marquis?" Cliché asked, straightening her skirt over her knees.

Marquis shot a look at me.

"First things first, Cliché," I interrupted.

The metal library door slammed open.

CHAPTER 17

THE ~~INTERVENTION~~ PEER MEDIATION

"Where's my burrito?"

Janie stomped into the library. Her eyes scanned the room, then the circle, then stopped on me.

"Zack," Janie swallowed, "what's going on? What are they all doing in here?"

"Come sit down next to me, dear." Mrs. Darling tapped the empty chair next to her. Her bracelets clanked against the blue plastic.

"What is this?"

"It's okay, Janie." I leaned toward her.

She sank into her chair next to Mrs. Darling.

"All right, Janie," I read from my notes. "We've all come together because we care about you, and we want to help you with your problem."

"You all know about the Nation's Best chocolate bars?"

Janie's voice became soft, and she looked to Mrs. Darling.

"Yes, dear, we all do, and we want to help you." Mrs. Darling nodded.

In silence, Janie looked around the room. "I . . . I . . ."

"We will help you, Janie," I cut her off. "All you need to do is *listen*."

"Did you figure out a way to come up with the money?" Janie said, looking down at her shoes.

"JUST LISTEN!" Sophia screamed. "UUUUUgh!" She turned away from Janie.

"Sophia, be gentle and caring." I pointed to my poster, bullet number one.

"I'm just being FIRM." Sophia stomped over to the poster and tapped her orange fingernail on bullet number six.

"FIRM, dear. This isn't a street fight; it's still a library." Mrs. Darling's right eye twitched.

Sophia pulled her skirt down and walked back to her seat.

"So far, I've found eighty-seven cents in my dad's recliner," Janie said.

"What's this about money?" Mrs. Darling asked.

I had left out the money part when I told Mrs. Darling about the peer mediation.

"The money for the chocolate bars," Janie explained.

"One hundred ninety-two dollars," Marquis said as he nodded.

"Well, Janie dear, we're here to talk about your problems." Mrs. Darling straightened her back. "That's why we are all here—to help you."

Janie spun toward Mrs. Darling. "Wait, are you going to help us pay for the candy bars?"

"Well, that's not really the point, Janie." Both Mrs. Darling's eyes twitched now.

"Well, Mrs. Darling," I added, "it wouldn't hurt."

Mrs. Darling's eye twitching sped up.

Nurse Patty's mouth kept opening like she was going to say something, but then she'd look at Mrs. Darling's twitching face and go silent.

I had to say something to get this intervention back on track, but my words got trapped in my throat again, like they always did.

"Maybe it's time we hear from our medical professional, Nurse Patty," Mrs. Darling managed to sputter out.

"Oh, uh, yes, well . . . have any of the rest of you had a problem like this?" Nurse Patty looked at each face in the circle, almost begging us with her eyes to respond.

But El Pollo Loco couldn't stand silence.

"Once I ate a whole value pack of Pop-Tarts—all sixteen of those brown sugar cinnamon ones from Walmart. My stomach swelled up like a tick on my dog, Donna." José stood up, stuck out his belly, and arched his back. "Aye, I was so full." He rubbed his belly with one hand and wiped his brow with the other.

"José, sit down," Mrs. Darling snapped.

"Oh"—El Pollo Loco pointed at Mrs. Darling's stomach—"did you eat a value pack of brown sugar cinnamon Pop-Tarts too, Miss?"

"Well," Mrs. Darling shifted in her chair, "now that you mention it. I did eat an entire Sara Lee cherry cheesecake once while it was still frozen, but that's not why we're here." She hit her knee with her hand. "We're here for Janie."

"And the money to pay for the chocolate bars Janie ate," Cliché said. "So we can have a dance."

"*You only have to be brave enough to see . . . MONEY!*" Janie stood. "*Brave*, two thousand twelve, starring Princess Merida."

"Mon-ey! Mon-ey!" Sophia and José started to chant and clap.

The others joined in.

"Zaaack!" Mrs. Darling yelled above the chanting and clapping. "That's not what you said this meeting was for when you asked for my help."

"MON-EY! MON-EY!"

"Well, we're going to help her, right?" I said, looking at the chanting circle.

Janie yelled, "Mon-ey. Mon-ey!" She stood on a chair and led the chant, raising her fist like she was some sort of protester on the news.

Mrs. Darling went over and started flashing the lights on and off to calm us down.

"Get DOWN, Janie!" I yelled.

She hopped off the chair and sat.

The chanting died down.

"Tell her how you feel." I looked up from my notes to the circle. I pointed to bullet number four and read: "*Explain how worried you are and how the teen's actions affect you.*"

"Yeah, I feel that I have been looking forward to going

to this dance with Raymond since I was in sixth grade the first time," Sophia said, stretching pink bubble gum in and out of her mouth. "And I already picked out some of Mom's clothes to wear to the dance, and I look good." She raised her eyebrows. She stood up and started to raise the roof with her arms, "So we gotta fix this, right?"

"FIX IT! *Right?* FIX IT! *Right?*"

Everyone started clapping and chanting louder and louder, and El Pollo Loco started dancing, shaking his booty to the left when he yelled, "FIX IT," and to the right when he yelled, "*Right?*"

"FIX IT!" Sophia shot her hips to the left.

"*Right?*" Their hips flew to the right.

"FIX IT! *Right?*"

Janie stood up on a chair again and whistled through her fingers like a man at a boxing match.

Nurse Patty shut her eyes and leaned back in her chair. The intervention needed an intervention.

CHAPTER 18
GETTING REAL

I stood up on a chair. "BE QUI-I-I-ET!"

The chanting stopped, the lights stopped flashing, and the circle sat.

"Look," I lowered my voice, "it's for the dance."

Nurse Patty checked her watch like she had somewhere else to be.

Mrs. Darling left her post at the light switch and joined the circle again.

"Tell her how you feel." I looked around at each face and stopped on Cliché.

Cliché stood. "I have never been to a dance, and I *feel* I want to go with someone special." She turned to Marquis and smiled.

Marquis spun the metal wing nut on his crutches.

"Tell her how it hurts you, dear," Mrs. Darling said.

"If we don't have the dance, I'll die. Janie, your eating too many chocolate bars hurts me by keeping me from going to the dance with . . ." She eyed Marquis, letting him complete her sentence.

But he'd gone into shy mode, like his face computer had crashed.

The intervention wasn't happening the way the TOO MUCH website had said it would.

El Pollo Loco took a deep breath, and for once he was surprisingly still. "Another time, I ate my little sister Esme's entire birthday cake." José stared forward. "And I blamed it on my dog, Donna." El Pollo Loco wasn't joking as usual. He was being honest.

The circle nodded.

A tear formed in his eye. Seriously.

"Then, Mom took Donna to Brackenridge Park and left her there." José swallowed. "I really miss that dog."

José dropped into his chair, staring at the center of the circle where a carpet square was peeling up.

"I never told anyone that." He bit his lip.

The intervention circle clapped like they were at a golf game or church. They were finally being respectful.

José wiped his eyes with the sides of his hands.

Sophia brought him a tissue.

"I used to eat handfuls of gummy vitamins," Marquis rubbed his nose, "until Ma figured it out and told me she'd tan my hide if I did it again."

"Isn't your hide already tan?" José blew his nose— *HONK!*

"Sometimes I eat Bonne Bell Dr. Pepper lip gloss for

breakfast on the bus," Sophia admitted.

Janie twisted her face as Sophia spoke.

José tried to return the tissue, but Sophia shook her head no.

Before I realized it, after only a few seconds of silence, I was the one spilling my guts. "Yesterday I ate a whole jar of Dollar-Store Pe-nutt Sandwich Spread." I pushed my hands in my pocket.

"Zack!" Janie leaned forward. "I think that has horse glue in it. I saw it on the Troubleshooters last night on the Channel 4 news."

I gazed back at her.

No one said a word—not even El Pollo Loco.

The silence.

The calmness.

It must have meant something to Janie.

No yelling.

No blaming.

No bullying.

"I ate the Nation's Best chocolate bars," Janie said, scratching her puffy cheek, "one at a time. I knew it was wrong, but I couldn't stop. I kept thinking, just one more, then I'll stop." She pulled her hair behind her ear. "Right after this one."

Each person in the circle nodded.

"Then, one more couldn't hurt." Janie shrugged. "Then, you've already eaten a box, why stop now? I'm so sorry. Really. I didn't mean to cause you all this trouble. Any of you." She wiped a tear from her eye, unable to look at us.

Mrs. Darling reached out her hand, "You poor dear. You know, once I ate an entire tray of cinnamon rolls sitting in my car in the Target parking lot."

"Some mornings"—Nurse Patty leaned into the circle—"I get into my car and get biscuits and gravy at the Whataburger drive-thru, even though I've already eaten breakfast at home with my husband. I eat them in my car before I come into the clinic."

"Once I found an old french fry between the seats of my dad's SUV," Cliché said. "And I ate it." She squeezed her eyes shut.

All this talk about eating in cars got me thinking. The answer was right there in front of us. TOO MUCH was right. And in a weird way, Janie was right too when she talked about telling the truth in movies. Everything did work out when you were honest.

We needed money.

Everybody had cars.

And we could take care of everything over the weekend.

"I have an idea," I mumbled.

But everyone kept talking.

I stood up on my chair and let it all out.

"For real. I can save the dance!"

CHAPTER 19
THE PLAN

Friday morning, in front of the lockers near the cafeteria, Marquis and I handed out fliers about the car wash. Dad had helped me make them on the Instant Lube copier. The flier had directions to the Instant Lube, site of the first-ever sixth-grade car wash this Saturday. Or as I called it: the *this-better-work-or-I'm-a-piñata* car wash.

The night before, I'd asked Dad if we could have a fund-raiser for the dance at the Instant Lube. I mean it really was for the dance, so I didn't lie by not explaining about the chocolate bar emergency.

Dad said he'd be proud to help with our school fund-raiser. "I like giving back to the community. Just like you're doing, Zack," he'd beamed. He'd also added, "As long as I'm not in charge, because I have to run the shop."

"Don't worry, Dad, you won't have to be in charge." Sure, I didn't explain absolutely everything. I didn't mention that he was saving my piñata. I also didn't tell him we didn't have an adult to be in charge yet. Mrs. Darling and Nurse Patty both had said they had "previous engagements"—whatever that means. And both had said I needed adult supervision. I figured since only adults can drive, we'd have plenty of adults at a car wash. Besides, Dad was happy because I was so involved in helping out the school. Luckily, he didn't ruin it by asking too many questions.

And seriously, it was just a car wash. What could happen? I mean, it was a group of middle school kids, water, soap, and . . . cars.

I gulped.

Raymond strolled past us. *Someday, I will walk that cool,* I thought.

"Hey, R-R-Raymond," I stuttered.

"What, small fry?" Raymond stopped.

I slowly lifted a flier toward him. "H-here's a flier for the car wash on Saturday."

Raymond grabbed it.

"Cool. Sophia already told me all about it. We'll be there." Then he strutted down the hall, folding the flier in half and sticking it in his back pocket.

"Yeah, I figure he can wash and dry the car roofs," I whispered to Marquis.

Cliché walked up, "Hello, Marquis."

Marquis just stood there, looking at his bandaged foot.

I kicked the bottom of his crutch. "Hand her the flier."

"I'm bringing the soap and a five-gallon pickle tub to mix soapy water in." Cliché took a flier.

I kicked his crutch again.

"Good."

I kicked his crutch again.

"Ouch," Marquis winced.

I glared at him.

"Well, we'll see you there then, Cliché."

After we handed out all the fliers, we told everybody to spread the word about the sixth-grade car wash, so kids could help or bring their parents to get their cars washed.

Marquis, Mr. Numbers, volunteered to take care of the money, since he couldn't get his bandage wet.

In third period, Mrs. Harrington said she'd bring her minivan by to get it washed. I guessed she forgave us for the Punctuation Day disaster because Cliché had written an apology letter on Mrs. Harrington's whiteboard. And, of course, it was persuasive and she used every punctuation mark to make sure Mrs. Harrington would know we meant it.

Mrs. Darling gave us her extra-long garden hose and sprayer from home, so we'd have something to rinse off the cars with.

Dad said we could use the Instant Lube's faucet. He even offered to tell everyone who got an oil change to get their car washed while they waited for an open bay.

Everybody helped.

Except for El Pollo Loco.

He said he wasn't even sure if he'd come to the car wash.

Seriously.

Cliché told us she was spending the night at Sophia's house. They promised to make posters to advertise the car wash.

MMMm

That night, I couldn't sleep. Without waking Dad, I snuck into the living room. Lying on the scratchy couch, I dialed Marquis's number and grabbed the remote while the phone rang. Earlier on the bus he'd told me Ma had to work the night shift.

I clicked on our new flat screen and channel surfed.

Marquis picked up.

"Hey, Marquis," I whispered. "Are you awake?"

"I am now," Marquis said. "But before I went to sleep, I calculated how many cars we need to wash tomorrow."

I wasn't finding anything interesting on TV. "Lay it on me," I said.

"We need to wash forty cars at five dollars each to make enough money to pay off the candy Janie ate."

I stopped on a channel with a bunch of teenagers on a camping trip in the woods. This had to be a horror movie. I set down the remote on my chest. The park ranger was watching the campers. I forgot to answer Marquis.

"Do you think we'll get forty cars, Zack?"

I gasped when the ranger pulled out a big machete!

"It's not *that* many," Marquis said.

The park ranger crept up to the campers' tents after they went inside.

"Well, tomorrow's the big day," Marquis said.

"Don't go to sleep!" I yelled at the clueless campers on the flat screen.

"I'm not, Zack. I'm right here."

I pushed my bare feet into the arm of the couch when the campers were saved by a hot dog commercial.

"Zack?"

"Yeah?" I looked up at the spinning ceiling fan.

"Do you ever get nervous around girls?"

"I get nervous around everybody."

"No, I'm serious."

"Is this about you asking Cliché to the dance?" I flexed my toes. "You could ask her at the car wash tomorrow."

"It's going to be tomorrow in two and a half minutes."

"Don't change the subject." I watched a commercial for a paycheck cashing store.

"I don't know," Marquis sighed. "What if she says no?"

The movie was back on. Now the girl who had gone to the bathroom was back looking for her friends.

"Don't do it." My knees lifted to my chest.

"You don't think I should?"

The girl on TV was walking toward the park ranger's SUV, and you could see bloody smudges on the door handle.

"Do you think Cliché would say yes?"

The park ranger jumped out of the door. "NOOOOOOO!" I whisper-yelled.

"Okay, Zack. Calm down. You really think she'll say no?"

I clicked off the TV and sat up. "No, I don't. I mean yes.

I mean I don't know what I mean, Marquis."

"Well, I don't know either."

"I only have ten percent battery left." I stretched out and closed my eyes.

"I only have ten percent brain left."

"Marquis?"

"What?"

"What if it rains tomorrow?"

"Then it will clear up and people will have dirty cars that need to be washed."

I sat there silently and rested my eyes.

"You worried?"

"Just tell me it's going to be okay, that everybody will actually show up." I couldn't open my eyes again.

"It's going to be okay."

I drifted off.

wmmn

The next thing I knew Dad was waking me up.

"Rise and shine, it's the big day."

CHAPTER 20
THE BIG DAY

SWEET RIDE

O n Saturday morning, Dad and I rode to the Instant
Lube together. He sipped coffee as he drove, and I
guzzled a Texas Teacup full of Coke. I held it between
my legs on the seat because it was too big for the cup holder.
We'd stopped at Bill Miller's on the way for egg and potato
breakfast tacos—two workingmen.

"I wish *I* could wear shorts to work." Dad set his coffee
in the cup holder.

"Well, I wish *I* could get a paycheck." I lightly socked
his arm. "So we're even."

We pulled into the empty Instant Lube parking lot.

"It's seven thirty on the dot, as promised, big man,"
Dad said. Dad knew I had to be on time, because I'd told
him that over and over while we were getting ready.

Janie came out from behind the big brown Dumpster

in the parking lot. She wore tan coveralls and had stuffed her hair into a black Spurs baseball cap with paint splattered on it.

"I've got it from here, Dad." I opened the creaky van door.

"Hey, son"—Dad lifted his chin at me, like cool guys do to each other—"see you after work."

"Sure thing," I said, rocking my head back in reply. "I got this."

"I know, Zack."

I shut the door and slung the wound-up green hose over my shoulder. I saw my reflection in the van window. I looked like a car-wash warrior. Dad waved. I waved back as he ground the van in gear and parked behind the shop.

I walked across the black asphalt toward Janie.

"I brought these masks from my dad's paint jobs," Janie said. She dropped a grocery sack full at my feet.

"Thanks for being here early." I set the Coke and hose on the pavement. "I hope Marquis gets here soon." He was bringing a table, a chair, and the towels to dry off the cars.

I rustled through the sack of white masks that would cover your nose and mouth, unsure how we could use them.

"Where's everybody else?" Janie looked around.

"They'll be here," I said.

I wondered if we could dry the cars with the paper masks.

We walked to the curb of San Pedro Avenue and looked up and down. Not a car in sight.

"I'll be right back." I went over to the side of the Instant

Lube to hook up the hose. As I finished tightening it, an ancient black Lincoln pulled up. Marquis was hanging out the window, waving. He wore a Hawaiian shirt and sunglasses. Marquis shoved open the Lincoln's door with his good leg and hobbled over on one crutch, carrying an empty pencil box in his free hand.

"Hey," I yelled. "What happened to your other crutch?"

"I'm so good, I only need one now." He bobbed his head like a funky chicken. "But I need you to get my chair and table out of the backseat."

"Oh, yeah? Exactly how long are you going to milk this crutch thing, Chicken Head?" I walked over to the Lincoln.

"As long as I can." He looked through his sunglasses. "And it's *Mr. Rooster* Head to you."

"Anything else, One Crutch Kid?"

"Yep," Marquis said. "Ma loaded up the trunk with a bunch of towels."

"I was joking," I said, grabbing the folding table.

"I'm on it," Janie shouted and huffed toward the trunk. And no one even asked her to help. She just did.

Ma didn't have to get out of the car, which was a good thing because she always complained about working on her feet all day.

Marquis selected a spot for the cash table and pointed to where I should unfold it.

After that, he sat down and placed the pencil box just so on the card table. I watched him line up a calculator, a yellow pad, and a mechanical pencil. Once he thought everything was straight enough, he looked up.

"It's almost eight. Where is everybody, Boss?"

"He's talking to you, Zack," Janie said, running her hands over the towels she had stacked in piles of five by the table.

"They'll be here." A green truck was coming down the street, but it drove past as did the car after it. "You heard them." My voice faded off.

"Good luck, kids!" Dad yelled across the parking lot to us, cupping his hand.

We smiled and waved back.

I gave Dad a thumbs-up, and he gave one back.

It was actually good we didn't have any customers yet. We were still missing the soap, a bucket, and the signs that would tell customers why we were standing around in the Instant Lube parking lot.

I paced back and forth, wandered to the faucet, checked the hose connection, then walked back to Marquis's table.

"What time is it now?" I drummed my fingers on the card table.

"Eight nineteen," Marquis answered, checking his watch.

A horn blasted as a light-gold Chevy van rolled up in the parking lot. I could see Sophia's mom driving. Actually, I was pretty sure Ms. Segura's eye makeup could have been seen from space.

"Let's get this wash on!" Ms. Segura hollered, blasting her horn again. Ms. Segura's first name was airbrushed on the side: DORITA. The *a* in DORITA turned into fluffy, white crashing waves.

Dad leaned out of the car bay, wiping his hands on a red rag, checking out the commotion. I waved him off. He nodded and disappeared into his shop.

Our first adult had arrived.

The passenger door of the van creaked open. Sophia emerged decked out in her red-and-black cheerleader uniform, with a pom-pom clutched in each hand. She even had those shiny metallic ribbons in her hair, reflecting light all over.

"*Ejole!* Wow," Janie said.

Sophia cleared her throat. "Ready, okay?" She shook her black-and-red pom-poms and cheered: "Soap 'em up! Rinse 'em off! *Way* off!"

"That's way off for sure," Janie said under her breath.

"Go-o-o-o-O, Alamos!" Sophia landed on the pavement in the splits, both arms up, pom-poms shimmering in the morning sun.

Marquis looked up from his calculator. "She's got spirit. Yes, she do. She's got spirit, how 'bout you?"

Janie and I stared at Marquis.

"What?" Marquis threw up his hands.

The side door of the van creaked open. Cliché popped out with a bucket and soap, and Raymond followed.

"Where are the customers?" Ms. Segura looked around, smacking her gum.

"Would you like your van washed, ma'am?"

"Oh, do I get to be the first customer?" She touched her hand to her leopard print top. "What an honor!"

She looked around. "Where are the beautiful signs you and Chi Chi made, *mija*?"

"I asked you not to call me that." Cliché slammed her bucket down on the pavement.

Without a word, Raymond leaned into the van and

came out with the signs—he's got that strong-silent-type thing down. Sophia read the sign in a cheer: "CAR WASH! Five Dollars! Help Davy Crockett Middle School Dance!" But this time she skipped the splits.

The message was simple, that's for sure. But it made the point. There was a gold glitter Alamo at the bottom that added sparkle. And to top it off, a puff of loose gold glitter fell off the Alamo every time the sign moved, giving it special effects.

"If y'all want customers, you have to get these signs on the street, *mija*," Ms. Segura said.

"My hands are full already. I've got a pom in each one." Sophia proved it by shaking each pom-pom.

"I'm out." Chi Chi, aka Cliché, kneeled and filled the empty five-gallon pickle tub with the hose and mixed in a squeeze of dishwashing soap.

"I'll hold the sign for you, *mija*. Give me a sec."

I began spraying off the side of Ms. Segura's van.

"Be careful, don't spray my pretty seascape off, *mijo*. It's airbrushed," Ms. Segura announced proudly. "I got that done custom from a guy at the flea market!"

"We'll treat it right, ma'am," I said.

wwww

After we finished, I looked around for Ms. Segura so she could pay. I walked to the card table. "Marquis, have you seen Sophia's mom?"

Marquis pointed his crutch toward the street. On the curb, Ms. Segura waved the sign at the cars. Cars honked. Sophia twirled and cheered. Two cars' tires squealed as they turned into the parking lot. Ms. Segura and Sophia jumped up and down like we'd just scored a touchdown. Our own car wash cheerleading team. It was official: we had a line.

wwww

Big cars, little cars, trucks, SUVs came one after the other. We washed them in an assembly line. Cliché took the bottom halves, and Raymond and some of his football-player friends cleaned off the tops. José decided to show up. But why, I don't know. He wasn't washing cars. He was trying to dance the Worm on the wet pavement, and I rinsed the soap off the cars. Janie did whatever else was needed, but soon she became the official dryer.

"I'm going to finish this car off like a bag of Doritos." She wiped away, making tight little circles like a towel ninja.

I had to face it. Janie worked harder than anyone else to fix this mess. I had to give her credit.

Unexpectedly, at about nine o'clock, Chewy and some other sixth graders I didn't really know showed up all at once to help. *This car wash just might work*, I thought to myself.

"Where's the bathroom?" Chewy asked.

"Use the one in the shop over there."

"Who's in charge?" a guy in a black Spurs T-shirt asked.

"That'd be me." I straightened up. You could say I was owning it. I pointed over to Janie, who looked up from drying the bumper of a station wagon. "Janie, here's your drying team. You're in charge."

Janie saluted me. "Aye, aye, sir. We won't let you down."

Her team quickly went through the mounds of towels Marquis's grandma had brought.

Janie really hustled. "Let's see if we can beat our time from the last drying job. Two minutes. Go!" Then, Janie blew a whistle. Where'd she get a whistle?

"I don't know about that whistle, but she's really killing it today," Marquis said.

Cars lined up and moved through our assembly line like a flowing river, and cash flooded the pencil box.

Marquis fanned himself with a handful of bills, laughing in his cartoon villain deep laugh, "*Bwah ha ha ha*! Only one hundred fifteen dollars to go."

I even had to pull Sophia and her mom off sign duty for an extra set of hands.

CHAPTER 21
A CHANCE FOR CASH

After a couple of hours of washing and drying cars, Mrs. Harrington's white minivan drove up. She looked different with sunglasses on. The minivan was coated in a layer of dust so thick it looked like she'd just driven across a desert. "Wash me" was written in the dirt layers down the side panel.

"Since this is a good cause," she pulled a wallet from her flowery quilted purse, "I'll pay you extra. How about fifteen dollars if you clean out the back of the van too?"

Sweet!

"With my three kids and teaching and grading essays, the last thing I have time for is cleaning my car." She counted out fifteen dollars into my hand. "I'm so embarrassed." She blushed. "It *really* is filthy."

"Cliché, you're in charge of cleaning out the back of Mrs. Harrington's minivan."

I wiped sweat from my forehead on the shoulder of my T-shirt.

"We'll make it as clean as a whistle," Cliché said.

Mrs. Harrington pressed a button on the minivan key to open the sliding door on the side. A grimy garbage avalanche slid to the asphalt: a half-eaten hamburger, a tennis shoe, a bunch of empty juice boxes, straws, a scratchy striped sweater, a basketful of dirty underwear, a folded-up diaper, and a ridiculous amount of Goldfish crackers.

"This is a pigsty," Cliché said, shaking her head.

"Shhhh!" I tilted my head toward Mrs. Harrington.

"Sometimes the truth hurts, Zack."

The aromas of the van began poisoning the air. José stopped dancing around and pinched his nose. "Aye, this reminds me of the compost heap my *abuelito* kept in his backyard."

"Okay, what if I give you twenty bucks?" Mrs. Harrington pulled out another five-dollar bill. "Will that do it?"

Now this lady is speaking, Zack, I thought. We needed that money. I smiled at Cliché, lifting my eyebrow to my scalp.

But Cliché wasn't having any of it. "I'm sorry, Zack. It's my break time." Cliché turned and walked over to the Car Wash Cabana that Sophia had begun fixing up with used wet towels.

I didn't know what to do. Everybody else had a job.

Janie took off her hat, turned the bill of her cap to the

back, and walked right up to Mrs. Harrington, circling her as she spoke.

"*Of all the* car washes *in all the world, she* drives *into mine.* Inspired by *Casablanca*, nineteen forty-two, starring Mr. Humphrey Bogart."

As Janie placed her foot on the garbage pile, she slid back a bit. But somehow she managed to balance long enough to stick her head in the minivan.

She popped her head back out. "This is my destiny."

"Thank you so much, kids." Mrs. Harrington sighed. "I'm so impressed with your cooperation." She shook all of our hands, even the soapy and wet ones—but not Janie's. She was too busy slipping on one of the masks she'd brought. Then she yanked a pair of white rubber gloves from her coverall pocket. The gloves snapped as she pulled them over her hands. Janie looked like some kind of garbage surgeon about to operate on Mrs. Harrington's messy minivan.

"I need trash bags. Lots of trash bags. Stat!" Janie held both gloved hands up like a doctor entering the operating room.

I borrowed a few industrial-sized trash bags from Dad.

Janie plowed through the debris, ridding the van of all that was not bolted down. "This is even worse than my dad's all-night poker parties." Her muffled voice rang out from the van.

"Hey, small fry, this is fun," said Raymond, wiping down the minivan roof, coolly stepping out of the way as trash flew from every opening in Mrs. Harrington's van. "Thanks for setting this up, so my girl Sophia can come to the dance with me."

"We only have sixty-five dollars to go," Marquis announced from his table, tapping on the pencil box. "*Bwa ha haha!*"

I giggled.

But like Cliché always said, "Don't count your chickens before they've hatched."

And as quickly as the river of cars began, they slowed. First to a trickle, then a drip, then totally dry.

"I'm bored," Chewy Johnson said. He'd already used the Instant Lube bathroom more than the rest of us combined.

"Yeah, this is boring, Zack," another sixth grader said. "We're leaving."

We were so close. But without cars, without a crew, we weren't going to make that last bit of money. Everyone was slumped over and thirsty, dry towels were running low, and kids were calling their parents to pick them up. Even Sophia's mother left to do some errands.

I had to do something. But what?

"Zack," Marquis said, grimacing, "I think I'm going to call Ma in a few. My foot's throbbing."

"Does she need her Lincoln washed?" I asked.

"Zack!" Cliché screamed. José was spraying Cliché with the hose. Water splashed the side of her face and soaked her down to her little white socks.

"I'm HOSE-A!" José held the hose above his head.

I ran over and yanked the hose away from El Pollo Loco, but not before he sprayed me too.

"You're all wet!" El Pollo Loco laughed. "Get it?"

Dripping, I dragged the hose across the cracked asphalt and dropped it by Marquis's table.

"Stop being a jerk, José!" Sophia handed Cliché a towel.

Then I sat on the hose, on the sprayer, which dripped. It wasn't comfortable or dry.

"Calm down, I was just trying to have some fun." José blinked rapidly.

The way Raymond looked at José I thought he was going to put the *fun* in funeral. José's.

The sun disappeared behind a cloud. The wind blew, and my soaked shirt felt like ice.

"I can stay a little longer," Marquis said.

I nodded, the sprayer poking my rear. The weight of the dance stuck to me like my soaked T-shirt to my back.

"Hey, *esé*," Raymond looked down at a soaked and crumpled me, "we are going across the street to the Church's Fried Chicken for a Coke."

"Sure. Why not?" I said with all the energy of a flat tire. Raymond and his eighth-grade friends swaggered off.

Defeated, I stared off at the others laughing in the Car Wash Cabana. We had gotten so close. José danced around making a fool of himself, and everybody watched. Wait. I had the perfect job for him.

"Hey, José!" I stood. "Come here."

"What for?" José asked, looking as if I planned to spray him with the hose.

"I noticed you've really got some dance moves."

"Well, yeah, everybody knows that." He chuckled, looking around.

"Why don't you work your magic with these signs?"

I held them up.

José grabbed one.

"Hey, Sophia, José is going to join you on sign duty," I said.

"No way!" Sophia barked, hands on hips.

"Come on, Sophia, the hose won't even reach the street," José reassured her.

Moments later a bright beam of sunlight came from behind the clouds and shone a spotlight on Sophia and José, dancing and spinning the signs as if they alone could make the clouds disappear.

CHAPTER 22
THE BIG BAD TRUCK

"WATER" BALLOONS

A black Chevy pickup truck crept into the Instant Lube parking lot, the loud muffler growling.

Chewy walked up beside me, blowing his nose. "Uh-oh."

"What's the matter?"

"This is gonna be trouble." Chewy dropped the tissue.

"Why?"

"That guy always drives around with his big high school punk friends picking on kids. One time they chased my brother and me, hurling eggs at us till we hid behind some big bushes." Chewy shook his head. "They like torturing middle school kids."

The dark tinted window of the pickup truck lowered: three huge high school guys were lined up across the front seat. Heavy metal music blared from the open window.

"I gotta go." Chewy backed away.

On his crutch, Marquis leaned his head down by the truck window. The driver turned down the music and said something. Marquis shrugged his shoulders and backed away. Nobody yelled. That was a good sign, right? But I couldn't hear anything over the muffler.

Then the driver motioned to the bed of the truck and laughed. Marquis walked over to it, and his face twisted up.

"Bam!" one of the boys yelled.

Marquis walked back to me with his head down.

"This guy told me we have to wash his truck for free— or else," Marquis said.

"Or else what?"

"He said if we don't do what he says," Marquis swallowed, "they'll throw water balloons of pee they've been filling all week. They have enough to get everybody here. I saw them in the back of the truck. And it really smells."

"Water balloons full of what?" My forehead wrinkled.

"Pee," Marquis whispered. "And he asked me if I wanted something to happen to my good leg."

I was confused. Who threatens kids like that? Who tries to steal a free car wash from a fund-raiser?

"I told him he had to talk to you because you're in charge. I didn't know what else to do."

The truck revved.

"We'll show you who's in charge!" yelled a bearded guy, sticking his head out of the truck. The guys doubled over laughing, and the driver mashed down on the horn.

Slowly, I stepped over to the honking truck. *I can do*

this, I repeated each time my foot hit the wet asphalt. *I can do this.*

"Hey, kid." The driver took a toothpick out of his mouth and pointed it at me, a string of slobber dangling from it. "You gonna wash my truck? I've been nice so far, but it seems like you're forcing me to come back and make a big mess. Is that what you want?" The whole time this creep talked, he looked around like he was deciding which one of us he'd take out first.

I didn't know what to say.

"How fast do you think your little friends can run?" He jutted his chin at the car-wash crew. "Oh, no! My foot's starting to slip off the brake," he taunted.

I sucked in a breath. I knew I had to tell him no, to stand up to him, to tell him to leave, but my voice stuck in my throat like I'd swallowed a jar of fake peanut butter— the plastic jar, the lid, all of it.

I turned to Marquis.

He shrugged from his chair.

Sophia and José walked back from the curb to see what was going on.

The truck engine revved again.

Somebody had to end this. I took a step back. My heart thumped loudly in my ear. *You be the change. You be the caboose.*

Pounding.

Pounding.

I pictured the balloons exploding all around us.

Oh, man, stranger danger, stop drop and roll, give a hoot don't pollute, take a bite out of crime, the more you know—every little save-the-day advice I'd ever heard flooded my brain till I drowned in worthless words.

"We're out of water," I blurted, taking a step away from the truck.

"*What?*" The driver sucked air in through his nose, revved his engine, and licked his chops like the big bad wolf or something.

"And towels. We're out of towels." It might have been convincing, except my voice broke.

"Just so you know, little man, you're forcing us to get the pee balloons out of the back of the truck and nail all you losers." The driver grinned. It seemed like this was the answer he was hoping for.

This was my last chance. This was go time. I had to pull out every last thing I had in me—all the way down to my Nikes. I swallowed hard and planted my feet on the pavement. And then the words came.

"Before you do, just so *you* know, that guy over there"—I pointed at Marquis—"he just memorized your license plate number."

"It's true." Marquis nodded. "I know my numbers."

"And see that girl over there?" I pointed at Janie. "She memorizes movie lines for fun." Janie tapped the side of her head, nodding. "She'll be able to quote, word for word, every threat you and your pals have made . . . to the police."

The guys in the truck glared at me, then Marquis, then at all the kids standing around watching.

"And Sophia. She's a cheerleader, and she knows how to get loud. She'll make so much noise, help will arrive before the first balloon hits the ground."

"Ready, okay?" Sophia struck an aggressive cheer pose, glaring.

I looked around for any other "threat," and my eyes landed on José. "Oh, yeah." I leaned in and with a loud whisper said, "See that guy over there?"

José stopped, with a who-me? face.

"They call him El Pollo Loco, because one time he got so mad at his *abuelo* that he strangled all his backyard chickens with his bare hands. All. Of. Them."

"Cockle DOODLE DO DO!" José cackled like a psycho, walking in circles.

Then all the kids—José, Cliché, Sophia, Janie, and even Raymond, who had just gotten back—stood behind me.

"We're closed," I announced. And I felt strong.

The driver glanced at his pals.

"Yeah, what Shrimps said!" Sophia took a step toward the truck, a pom-pom on each hip.

The truck's window rolled up.

"Yeah, you heard 'em. *Bwak! BWWAAK!*" El Pollo Loco squawked, like the crazy chicken he was.

The pickup truck's back wheels spun, spitting out loose gravel, peeling out of the parking lot. The metal scraped as the truck hit San Pedro, and a few balloons flew out and exploded on the street.

Dad ran over just in time to see the truck speeding away.

My legs melted, and I collapsed into Marquis's chair.

"Are you all okay?" Dad asked, out of breath, confused. "I heard all the noise, but it took me a second to get out of the bay."

"Zack saved the day," Cliché said.

"He went all Mighty Mouse or something," Raymond said, slapping his enormous hand on my shoulder.

"He told those creeps off," Sophia agreed.

"Yeah," Cliché said, looking at me, "you should have seen him, Mr. Delacruz."

"He really told 'em!" Janie said.

Dad took off his gray Instant Lube shirt, leaving his white T-shirt. "Here, son," he said, handing it to me. "Put this on. You're soaked." At that moment, I wasn't a hundred percent sure if my shirt was wet from José spraying me or from threatening the thugs.

"Is everybody okay?" Dad asked.

"Yes, because of Zack," José said.

Surprised, I looked at him. José had just backed me up. More than that, really.

"I'm staying until you earn the money you need," Dad said. "My guys can handle the shop for a while."

In the chair, I breathed in the sweet smell of oil from Dad's shirt.

Everybody sat down and started talking.

After a few minutes, I remembered we had a car wash to finish. I stood. "Okay, listen up, Fighting Alamos, we can do this." I looked at everybody. "We *will* do this. All we need is to wash twelve more cars, and we can make this dance happen. We'll make history at Davy Crockett Middle School." I was getting into it. "We will be the first sixth grade to attend the fall dance!"

The girls clapped and cheered, the boys patted me on the back, and Janie whistled through her fingers like only Janie could.

Sophia picked up her pom-poms, "Ready, okay?"
"Remember the Alamos!" Janie raised her fist.
"REMEMBER THE ALAMOS!" everybody cheered.

CHAPTER 23
THE TROUBLE NEVER ENDS

PRINCIPAL

ABANDON HOPE
ALL YE WHO
ENTER HERE

n the halls at school on the Monday morning after the car wash, I was surprised how many people talked to me. It was some kind of record.

"I heard you did good," a girl towering over me said. I didn't even know her.

"Hey, Mighty Mouse, I hear you saved the day this weekend," a seventh grader said as he walked past. That was still a step up from Enrique Potter.

"You're a celebrity." Marquis snapped photographs of me with an imaginary camera phone. I noticed that for the first time all year he wasn't wearing his warm-up jacket.

"Cut it out, goofball." I shoved him off balance.

"Zack." Marquis stopped smiling. "You've changed."

"Whatever." I slipped my backpack over my shoulder. "Let's go."

I knew Marquis was joking, but maybe I had changed. I had to admit, it wasn't so bad having people say hello to me in the hall. Strange, but not bad.

The car wash had made all the money we needed on Saturday afternoon. Sixth grade was excited about going to the Night at the Alamo fall dance, and everybody said I'd made it happen. But if I'd learned anything over the last couple of weeks, even when you do the right thing, it doesn't mean everybody's going to like it.

There would always be some haters. Already some seventh and eighth graders didn't think it was fair that *they* didn't get to go to the dance when *they* were in sixth grade.

"Boooo!" A football player made a thumbs-down sign as he passed.

"Keepin' you humble." Marquis patted my shoulder. "Keepin' you humble."

wWMm

But in the hallways that Monday, I knew it wasn't all over yet. I couldn't forget the fact that not everybody at school was happy about the car wash, even though we'd made the money back. When Dad had called Principal Akins after the car wash to let him know what'd happened, Mr. Akins had said I needed to stop by his office Monday at lunchtime for a conversation. A conversation? With Mr. Akins? At lunch?

I stopped by the library before classes to hand in the rest of the money for the fund-raiser.

Mrs. Darling was returning books to the shelves, sitting on the rolling library stool that looked like a tree stump.

"Hello, Zack." She looked up over half-glasses, which today were lemon yellow. "How'd the car wash go?"

I handed her the envelope and smiled. "It's all there."

"This is wonderful, Zack."

I kicked at the ground. "There's one more thing though."

"Well, don't leave me in suspense, Zack."

"Mr. Akins wants to see me."

"Oh my!" Mrs. Darling shelved a book and took a breath. "He might have a bee in his bonnet that you had a school event off campus without getting prior approval from him."

"But I don't even know what that is." I rubbed my forehead.

"Zack, I feel partly at fault." She got off the stool. "How about I accompany you to the meeting with Mr. Akins?"

"Really?"

"Of course, it's the least I could do." Mrs. Darling smiled.

Then, without thinking, I threw my arms around her and squeezed.

"It'll all be fine, Zack." She patted my back. "So, when is our meeting?"

uWWmn

After third period, Mrs. Darling met me outside Mr. Akins's open door. We traded looks like two scared kids accused of throwing rolls in the cafeteria.

I stood there, my hands in my pockets, rocking up and down on my toes.

"Just tell the truth, Mr. Delacruz." Mrs. Darling touched

my shoulder. "And that Zack Delacruz charm won't hurt either." She looked at her watch and straightened her hair.

Mr. Akins sat on his black office-chair throne, signing and moving papers around to different stacks. I didn't think he was ever going to look up, and that was fine with me. His white bullhorn was on his desk too. I hoped he wasn't planning on yelling at me with it.

"Knock, knock!" Mrs. Darling sang.

"Come in and have a seat." Mr. Akins straightened a stack of papers on his desk. "I'll seek to be with you both momentarily."

"Thank you, sir." I bowed my head.

I gave Mrs. Darling my "how'd-you-like-that?" face.

But Mrs. Darling eyed the chair.

I sat.

I could tell Mrs. Darling believed in me. Marquis did too. And Mom and Dad believed in me. But in that moment, I didn't know why any of them did.

It was the first time in my life I'd been in the principal's office.

Well, except for a tour we took in kindergarten.

I glanced around at the walls of Mr. Akins's office. I stopped on a poster framed in black: *What's popular isn't always right, but what's right isn't always popular.* I thought I'd try to work that into our conversation.

After a few minutes, Mr. Akins leaned back on his throne and crossed his shiny black shoe over his left knee. "Now, Mr. Delacruz, I'd like for you to seek to tell me your version of the events that transpired during the unfortunate incident at the car wash this past Saturday."

Mr. Akins listened as I apologized. When he nodded, the light glinted off his bald head.

"Mr. Delacruz, it is first and foremost my duty to inform you that district policy states that any school-sponsored, off-campus event must seek prior approval from the principal before proceeding."

"Oh, it wasn't really a school-sponsored event. It was more of a me-sponsored car wash." I shrugged. "It was at my dad's work."

"But, you'd acknowledge it was a fund-raiser for Davy Crockett Middle School sixth graders to seek to participate in the fall dance?" He lowered both his chins and waited.

"Yes?" I turned to Mrs. Darling. I wondered if he was a lawyer.

"Zack may not have had a full understanding of this regulation, and he may have been under the impression that it was okay."

"Please explain."

"I knew they were planning on having a car wash, and I knew about the rule, so if anyone should be in trouble, it's me." Mrs. Darling shrugged.

"Mrs. Darling, the two of us shall convene that conversation at a later time."

Right then, I decided to offer to come with her, like she'd done for me.

He turned back to me. "Have you given any thought to all of the possible problems that could have arisen for *studens*, due to your failing to follow district policy?"

"Uh . . ."

He touched his thick fingers as he listed all the bad stuff

that could've happened: "Bodily injury, huge lawsuits, untimely deaths, heatstroke."

Nodding, I got distracted by his bald head. I wondered if he waxed it to get it that shiny.

"So, the question of the day is, why were you having this car wash in the first place?"

"One of the students—let's call her Janie Doe," I leaned on Mr. Akins desk for support, "checked out eight boxes of Nation's Best chocolate bars, and let's say she ate every last one of them."

Mr. Akins's eyes widened and darted to Mrs. Darling.

"And tell him what you did to fix the problem, Zack." Mrs. Darling cleared her throat.

"Well, we had this interven—"

Mrs. Darling interrupted, patting my knee. "Zack organized a car wash to raise the money to help the student out."

"Janie Doe?" Mr. Akins asked.

"Sure, let's call her *Janie.*"

I spilled every last detail (except for the intervention) on the big wooden desk, piled with papers.

"I very much appreciate your father calling me Saturday night to give me a heads-up," Mr. Akins said, nodding.

I leaned back.

"That was absolutely the right thing to do in such a situation." Mr. Akins held up his finger. "One truth has served me well throughout my life: when you mess up, you fess up."

"And let's not forget, under Zack's leadership, the students completely made back the money to support a fellow student," Mrs. Darling said, sitting up straighter, "which I think shows admirable initiative and compassion."

"What is right isn't always popular," I mumbled.

Mr. Akins looked over his shoulder at the framed poster behind him and nodded.

"Yes, indeed, Mr. Delacruz."

"You know, the weird thing is, it really is just like that sign says." I leaned forward on his desk. "If you do something right and everybody likes what you did, you're a hero. If you do something right and people don't like what you did, you're a loser."

Blinking, he looked at me for a minute. He drew in a deep breath and laced his fingers behind his head. "Sounds like you learned something, young man."

I kept waiting for him to say the sixth graders wouldn't be able to go to the dance. But he never did.

"Well, Mr. Delacruz, I am not happy at all with this unfortunate situation. However, I am impressed with your sincere apology and your superior problem-solving capabilities. What I see in you is a leader, Mr. Delacruz." Mr. Akins raised his finger in the air again. "*A leader knows the way, goes the way, and shows the way.*"

"Those were some powerful words"—Mrs. Darling looked to me—"weren't they, dear?"

"Yeah, they rhymed and everything," I said.

"What do you think the lesson is in all of this hubbub, Mr. Delacruz?" Mr. Akins asked, rocking forward, his big leather chair creaking.

"Always get prior approval?"

"Always." Mr. Akins smiled and grabbed his bullhorn.

"I have to get to the cafeteria."

Mrs. Darling and I stood, and Mr. Akins shook my hand, gripping it tight like a vice from Dad's shop.

"You have a good school, Mr. Akins." Rubbing my hand, I winked at Mrs. Darling. That was all part of the Zack Delacruz charm that Mrs. Darling had talked about.

Still, for the next few days, I couldn't shake the feeling that an announcement would be made that the sixth grade could no longer attend the dance.

But it never was.

CHAPTER 24

READY OR NOT

Friday—the day of the Night at the Alamo dance—finally arrived.

I'd been living with my mom since Sunday. And because it was the week leading up to the dance, I'd become Mom's extreme makeover project. I was like a house she needed to fix up and sell fast. I guessed she wanted me to have a date or something.

"I just want to spruce you up a bit, Zack." Mom licked her finger and straightened my spikes into some kind of part.

"Mom!" I smacked her slobbery hand away and poured my bowl of Cheerios—the real kind.

"If it's my week to be your mother, then by golly, this week I'll be your mother." She put on her lipstick while I ate my Cheerios. "You need to be ready in ten."

At the breakfast table, I thought about the past week—
Makeover Week: Zack Edition—as I crunched on my cereal.
If mothers were supposed to be a pain, then by golly mine
had been a real mother. Holy guacamole! A haircut. A new
navy-blue shirt that buttoned *and* had a collar (when all I
really wanted was a shirt without buttons or a collar). New
shoes. A new darker pair of jeans. At least I wouldn't have
to wear khakis for one day of my life!

wwwww

The day of the dance crept by like an endless multiple-
choice test.

Sophia and her clique came to school with big curlers in
their hair. Half the girls showed notes to Mrs. Harrington,
so they could go home after third period to get ready for
the dance.

When Cliché was packing up her stuff, she told
Marquis, "In case you have anything to ask me, here's my
number." She handed him a folded-up sheet. "I won't be
coming back until the dance at four thirty."

Marquis looked like a statue.

"O . . . kay, so if you need to ask me anything . . ."
Cliché paused, raising her eyebrows as she backed out of
Mrs. Harrington's door.

My afternoon classes were almost empty. The
teachers didn't want to do anything because so many kids
were gone. Teachers hated to give make-up assignments.
So, we had free time. At first I was afraid of the free
time because I always got bullied or tortured. But
today, free time felt . . . free. Marquis and I talked and

laughed. I didn't feel like I needed to be quiet and hide anymore. Sure, José asked, "Are you going to the dance with Janie?" But it was more like how Marquis or Dad teased me.

I wrote, *Why didn't you invite Cliché to the dance?* on a piece of notebook paper we'd been playing tic-tac-toe on. I wasn't hiding. I was asking something I wanted only Marquis to see.

"Who'd you ask, Zack?" Marquis waited. He didn't even bother to write back.

"Okay," I said. "I get why you didn't ask. But she would've said yes: I am one hundred percent sure."

"That's the problem." Marquis nodded. "She'd say yes, and then what?"

I hadn't thought about that.

Even when girls complimented my shirt today it made me feel like something was wrong with me. (Okay, so what if the "girls" were Mom, Mrs. Darling, and Mrs. Harrington—a compliment is a compliment.)

"I guess sometimes you actually have to *do* something before you can find out what will happen when you do." I stared out the window at the PTA ladies unloading boxes of dance decorations from their cars.

"Like Ma says, 'Start small.'"

"What's that mean?" I turned back.

"It means," Marquis said, "I'll ask her for *one* dance."

"One?"

Marquis snapped back, "Zack, how many times are you asking anyone to—"

"Okay," I interrupted. "Okay."

I'd worried so much about the dance happening that I'd forgotten to worry about who I'd ask to dance.

Or how.

Or if.

Who would say yes to *me*?

And what would I do if she said no?

I took a deep breath.

Like Ma says, start small.

CHAPTER 25

EL POLLO LOCO

By four thirty, the cafeteria had almost been transformed into A Night at the Alamo. But the lights were still on. The rows of lunch tables were folded up and wheeled against the wall. Colored butcher paper covered the wall of windows that faced the courtyard, blocking out the afternoon sun.

Mrs. Darling was so busy taping little orange, brown, and red Alamo cutouts on the walls she didn't see me. On a ladder, Coach Ostraticki finished taping strings of Christmas lights on the cinder block. He wore some kind of dress tracksuit—white velour with a black tie. His mustache looked ready for the dance.

He looked down from the ladder. "Is that you, Delacruz?"

What now? I thought.

"You look downright spiffy, kid." He climbed down the ladder.

"Indeed," Mrs. Darling agreed.

Unsure of what to say, I spun away and got tangled in the streamers that dangled from the ceiling tiles. My new shoes slid a little on the glitter that had been sprinkled all over the floor. Once I got my balance, I spit a piece of streamer out of my mouth and looked around for Marquis.

"All right, I need everybody's attention," Mrs. Harrington said into a microphone from the stage. "It's a few minutes past four thirty, so I'd say this dance has officially started." She waved her hand to Mr. Akins, who turned off the cafeteria lights with a key. "Let the dancing begin!" Everybody cheered. Music started pounding.

The smell of Axe body spray, pizza, and nerves filled the air. I had to admit it: I was disappointed no one had worn a coonskin cap to the Night at the Alamo dance.

As I was making my second loop around the cafeteria, I wondered where I was supposed to put my hands. I stood there trying to look cool, moving my hands in and out of my pockets.

I decided to hold my arms out to the side, my hands hovering over each of my pockets.

"Are your arms okay, Mr. Delacruz?" Mr. Akins asked. "It looks like you're seeking to draw six-shooters."

My hands slipped into my pockets. "Well, I couldn't afford a coonskin cap, so . . ."

As I tried to get a safe distance from Mr. Akins, a new worry attacked: Do you take your hands out when you walk or leave them in? And how come I never really thought about this till now?

Our math teacher, Mr. Gonzalez, stood at the door drinking a can of Diet Coke. The doors sprung open, and Marquis strolled in wearing one of his dad's old outfits that Ma had dug out of a box for him. His white pants shone. Striking a few model poses with his crutch, Marquis popped the collar of his burgundy satin shirt.

Mr. Gonzalez laughed so hard that soda trickled out of his nose and streamed down his striped tie. Diet Coke through our math teacher's nose! No wonder everyone wanted to go to the dance.

I ran to greet Marquis.

"Look around, my man," Marquis said. "This is all on you."

"I had some help."

We looked around.

"Yeah," I said, "it's not half bad in here. I barely recognize the cafeteria."

"How come the boys and girls are on different sides of the dance floor?" Marquis asked.

"I don't know. You're the expert on girls."

"I guess they're just waiting for someone to ask them to dance." Marquis bobbed his rooster head.

I shrugged.

Another song blasted from the tall black speakers by the DJ—who was really just Mrs. Gage, our lunchroom monitor. She was wearing a hat, sunglasses, and a man's tie over a white T-shirt.

The music pulsed louder and louder.

Mrs. Darling started swaying and tossing her red mop of hair back.

She turned and slid her feet backward, as if she were moon walking. She looked like a puffy cloud with a red Magic Marker tip.

"Oh, here it comes," Marquis said.

Mrs. Darling hooped her arms out in front of her, doing the Dougie again. She yelled to all those nearby, "Join me!" Nurse Patty and a few girls quickly made their way to the safety of the soda table.

Mrs. Darling scanned the crowd for her next dance victims.

"Don't make eye contact with her, Marquis!" I warned.

But it was too late.

"Marquis!" she shrieked with cupped hands. "Zaaaack! You must join me. It's simply divine!" Her pearl necklace bounced to the beat.

I looked at Marquis; he looked back.

We looked at his crutch.

We shrugged, then joined Mrs. Darling on the dance floor.

Near the end of the song, Mrs. Darling leaned in and shouted into my ear over the bass, "I am so glad I got to dance with the man of the hour."

I smiled, but before I could thank her, the doors flung open.

Sophia and Raymond entered the cafeteria.

Everybody stopped dancing, like it was Sophia's *quinceañera* and we were all supposed to clap in her honor.

But only Sophia's clique clapped. Sophia waved like

she was on a River Parade float.

José walked up behind us, wearing his uniform, even though he didn't have to. "Get a load of them." He pointed to the couple.

Sophia's dress was green and shiny, with a ruffle at the top.

"With those blonde highlights, she looks like a sunflower." José elbowed me. "Am I right, or am I right?"

Her arms shimmered with glitter makeup. Sophia reached her hand to Raymond's, who wore black tuxedo pants, a white jacket, and a black T-shirt.

José pointed to the refreshment table. "My brother told me the pizzas and the sodas are all you can eat."

Pepperoni pizza, cheese pizza, sausage pizza, veggie pizza, and every other pizza you can think of covered the two tables.

"*Dios mio.* I'm in heaven!" El Pollo Loco slapped both of his hands to the sides of his face. He looked at the columns of pizza boxes stacked behind the tables.

"That reminds me of the Nation's Best chocolate bar boxes," I said. "But we are supposed to eat these."

José grabbed a piece of pepperoni pizza out of one of the opened boxes, folded it in half, and chowed down. He didn't even get a plate.

"Eat up, boys," Nurse Patty said. "I know you worked hard to make this dance happen. But *please.* Do take a plate." She glared at José, pushing a white paper plate at him. "It's more sanitary."

wMMw

After a while, Mrs. Darling stopped dancing and plopped down at the soda station, removing her book-shaped earrings. "I'm getting too old for this." She fanned herself with a stack of white paper plates.

"Why would anyone ever leave the pizza table?" I said, picking up another slice that never even touched my plate.

"I know that's right," José said.

Nodding, I grabbed another slice of cheese pizza. A big hand gripped my shoulder.

I froze.

"Don't eat all my pizza, Mighty Mouse."

It was Raymond.

"AAAAh, snap!" he said. "But seriously, *holmes*, if you and your little sixth-grade friends eat up all our pizza," he tilted his head to the side and threw his arms open, "watch your back."

He and his friends piled pizza slices on white paper plates and strutted across the cafeteria, like they were downtown on the Riverwalk instead of at a middle school dance.

"Laters."

"I guess your run as big man on campus is over." Marquis tossed a crust in the trash.

"Yeah, I guess."

I spotted Cliché walking across the empty dance floor straight toward Marquis. Cliché wore a pink dress with a white sweater over it.

I punched Marquis's arm, and his mouth dropped open.

Her black hair was extra curly that night, and shiny. For the first time in history, she was without her little lace socks.

"Hi," he said, "I mean, good evening." He looked like he was about to take a bow.

"Hello." Cliché twisted a white pearl button on her sweater.

As a slow song started, Marquis extended his hand ever so slowly, and Cliché took it. They walked out to the middle of the cafeteria.

The three of them danced: Cliché, Marquis, and his crutch.

Still at the soda table guzzling more Big Red, El Pollo Loco let out a rumbling burp.

I wondered aloud, "Where's Janie?"

"Yeah, this is like church to her," José said. "She makes the sign of the fork every time she enters."

"José!"

"Yeah, yeah." José sighed.

El Pollo Loco ignored Raymond's warning and kept returning to the pizza table. His lips, stained red from all the soda, distracted your eyes from the tomato sauce splatter on his shirt. He didn't do much to help with the dance, but he was making sure there weren't going to be any leftovers to clean up. Maybe José had found a career that would build on his strengths: competitive eating. He looked over at me, pushed out his swollen belly, and rubbed it. "Aye, I need an intervention before I pop."

Funky accordion music blared from the speakers.

"It's the 'Chicken Dance'!" Mrs. Darling yelled.

"My song!" El Pollo Loco bounded into the center of the dance floor.

Mrs. Darling joined him. "Everyone form a circle, and

I'll show you what to do."

She stood in the middle of the circle, showing everybody the moves. She stomped and clapped, moved up, then back. We joined hands and repeated her moves, circling the cafeteria.

Clap. Clap.

And the best part was, sometimes you got to put thumbs in your armpits, flapping your arms like a chicken.

"Holy guacamole!" I laughed.

Chewy laughed so hard he had to leave the circle.

Mrs. Harrington couldn't help it—she looked at me and we both laughed.

Clap. Clap.

Mrs. Darling waved her hand inviting anyone else who wasn't part of the Chicken Dance mob yet. The circle got bigger and bigger—till everyone was in it—even our principal, Mr. Akins; Nurse Patty; and Mr. Gonzalez, with his Coke-stained tie.

Every time I messed up, I laughed so hard I could barely catch my breath.

Clap. Clap.

El Pollo Loco was doing his dance proud. When we shook our bottoms to the ground, El Pollo Loco shook his three times as much. When we moved across the floor, he moved three times as far. When we clapped our hands hard, he did it the hardest.

Sweat flung from his forehead as he chugged along. Then he broke away from everyone, joined Mrs. Darling in the center of the circle, and stopped.

"Get ready. This'll be good." I elbowed Marquis.

Clap. Clap.

Except El Pollo Loco stayed motionless—pale gray like a zombie. Then he started swaying slowly. His head pulled back like he was going to yell. His cheeks swelled, and he turned to Mrs. Darling.

Bluuuaaaak!

Partially chewed pizza and a few liters of Big Red soda gushed from El Pollo Loco's mouth like flames from a dragon. The long red stream flew toward Mrs. Darling, heading downward with force. She jumped high by lifting her knees. The vomit plume splattered on the floor beneath her. She hovered above the Big Red and pizza vomit, like she was doing some kind of *Matrix* limbo. Then, as her feet approached the tile floor, she threw both legs out to the side. After she landed, both arms went up to balance her.

The kids parted like the Red Sea.

Literally.

Bursting through the crowd, Coach Ostraticki ran to save Mrs. Darling. He slipped when he hit the puddle. Mrs. Darling spun away in a blur, crouching-tiger style. But Coach O. slid past her and slammed into the stage with a bang. Instantly his white velour began soaking up the foamy red vomit. A whole pepperoni piece stuck to his nose as he slipped and slid, trying to get up.

Mr. Akins clicked the lights on, and it was silent, except for the perky little accordion of "The Chicken Dance" playing on in the background.

CHAPTER 26
REMEMBER THE ALAMO

Mr. Akins used his bullhorn to direct us to the courtyard while Manny the custodian cleaned up José's biggest contribution to the dance.

After a while, Mrs. Harrington opened the glass doors and let us back into the cafeteria. Chewy Johnson pushed through, making his way for the bathroom. The lunchroom smelled sour, like a wet mop. I felt woozy. Ms. Segura and the other chaperones picked up paper plates, pizza boxes, and plastic cups.

With the lights back on, things looked less fresh, less colorful, less A Night at the Alamo, and more like the aftermath of a battle at the Alamo. The butcher paper covering the windows sagged, the masking tape having lost its grip. The glitter had mostly been mopped away.

The bass began thudding, and the lights dimmed. Marquis and Cliché started dancing. Again.

That night, sixth graders, seventh graders, and eighth graders danced together for the first time in the history of Davy Crockett Middle School. I looked around the room at all the faces. We were all here. Except Janie. After all the eating and car washing, not to mention the intervention, I couldn't blame her for not showing up.

I bent over to take a strip of damp crepe paper off my shoe. When I turned around to throw it away, it stuck to my finger. Sophia stood there, with her clique looking like her backup singers.

"Hey, Shrim—I mean Zack," Sophia said. "My mom told me I should thank you for all you did to help us get the dance, so thanks."

I kept trying to shake the wet paper off my hand.

She looked around. "This is really nice." She slipped her ring on and off. "See you in English."

"Yeah," I said, "see you . . . in English." The paper finally dropped to the floor, and the clique giggled as they returned to the dance floor.

Marquis would never believe it. I wanted to tell him, but he was still dancing with Cliché. Start small, huh? But now I think I understood what Ma had meant. You don't do things all at once; you do them a small step at a time.

El Pollo Loco came back through the cafeteria doors wearing a baggy school uniform. "Nurse Patty loaned it to me. She says she keeps them for accidents."

José flopped down on a metal folding chair by the door. "I'm gonna wait here till Mom gets off work."

I sat beside him.

"I'm hungry," José said.

"Seriously?" My eyebrows squished together.

"No." He smiled, leaning back. "You did all right, Zack." Then he drifted off to sleep, snoring with his mouth open, the *Siesta* Chicken.

I watched the dance. Raymond spun Sophia around like they were in a competition. The clique clapped. I rocked my head to the music.

A hand touched my shoulder.

I turned.

It was Janie: a purple flower in her hair, a shiny purple dress, even purple shoes.

The music stopped.

Mrs. Harrington tapped the microphone. "May I have your attention, please?"

We turned toward the stage.

"It's time for the last dance of the night," she said.

"Awww!"

"But before we do that"—she pulled back her hair—"I want to say a couple of things. First, everyone's okay." Mrs. Darling stood and waved. "As for Coach Ostraticki, when I helped him into his truck, he wanted me to tell you, since he can't be here, 'NO LOITERING. Everybody dance!'"

We cheered and clapped.

"We can't leave here tonight without acknowledging a few things. I want to thank Zack and all the kids who reminded me what it means to work together." She motioned toward José, Janie, me, then all the students. But everyone kept looking at the three of us.

Instead of feeling embarrassed or afraid, I felt happy and proud. And relieved that I didn't have to sell chocolate bars anymore. Relieved that I didn't have to disappear anymore. Relieved that I didn't think I really wanted to anymore. For the first time, I felt like everyone else. Not worse, not better. Just Zack.

"Let's give everybody a hand for cooperating when something needed to be done."

From the dance floor, Cliché and Marquis cupped their hands and yelled, "Zaaaack!" Maybe a few kids did yell "Shrimp!" when they clapped, but it didn't feel like an insult anymore. More like a nickname.

Mrs. Harrington adjusted the microphone. "Take a little picture with your mind right now. Enjoy this moment."

I tried to let it all sink in, but then the last song began.

"Zack, may I have this dance?" Janie asked.

"I thought you weren't going to come because of all that happened this week." I stayed seated, not answering but answering.

The entire cafeteria danced facing toward us. Even from his chair, El Pollo Loco cracked one eye open. Okay, so maybe sometimes I still might feel like disappearing.

"It sure looks like everyone's having fun out there." Janie stared forward, adjusting the purple flower in her hair.

"Yep," I said, rocking from heel to toe.

We stood next to each other, watching.

The car-wash crew formed a circle on the dance floor. Everybody waved at Janie and me to join.

I shrugged and turned to Janie. She shrugged back, and we walked toward the circle. To be honest, the circle wasn't really a circle—it was crooked and had big gaps. But for now, it was a sixth-grade kind of perfect. The ovalish blob danced, and I looked around at all the faces: Marquis and Cliché, Raymond and Sophia, the blue eye shadow gang. I couldn't believe we'd actually done it—the fund-raiser, the car wash, the dance—and it had taken each one of us.

And here we were.

Dancing.

No telling what could happen now.

THE ~~END~~ BEGINNING?

— ZACK

IN GRATITUDE

In Zack's story, relationships were key to accomplishing goals, and that's true for publication as well. First, I am indebted to my students. You made my life full and gave me much more than I ever gave you. To my colleagues in schools, I honor the delicate job you do providing a literate, meaningful future for all those who need it.

I am grateful for my writing community, which spans states and time: First and foremost, I thank the motivating and supportive Lola Schaefer and the accepting, wild, and inspiring Heather Miller. Writers need company: Thanks, Roseanne Wells (agent), Linda, Aimee, Tracy, Greg, Mark, and Donalyn.

The family at Sterling Children's Books makes the magic happen, and I adore them for it. To Brett Duquette, my editor, you're the mac to my cheese. Andrea Miller, your illustrations were psychic perfection. Lauren Tambini, Sari Lampert, Chris Vaccari, Zaneta Jung, Joshua Mrvos, Scott Amerman, Hanna Otero, and Theresa Thompson, thank you for getting this book into young hands.

And Terry, always Terry.